श्रेष्ठ भारतीय साहित्य

भारतीय ज्ञानपीठ

Oh, These Rehnumas!

(Novel)

Oh, These Rehnumas!

Original story by
Ms. Tasneem Khan

Translated by
Dr. Jyotika Elhance

Bharatiya Jnanpith

Lokoday Granthmala : Granthank 1478

ISBN 978-93-90659-59-3

OH, THESE REHNUMAS!
(Novel)
By Ms. Tasneem Khan

English Translation by
Dr. Jyotika Elhance

Cover : Maheshwar

Printed by : Bharatiya Jnanpith, New Delhi-3

Published by
Bharatiya Jnanpith
18, Institutional Area, Lodi Road, New Delhi-110 003
Ph. : 011-24698417, 24626467; 23241619 (Daryaganj)
Mob. : 9350536020; e-mail : bjnanpith@gmail.com
sales@jnanpith.net; website : www.jnanpith.net

First Edition : 2021
Price : Rs. 330

Dedicated to
My parents, my parents-in-law & my children

INTRODUCTION

Oh, These Rehnumas! is a heart-wrenching portrayal of those Muslim women who belong to an even more marginalized section of this minority community, and are bound by the shackles of the regressive patriarchal practices since time immemorial.

Taha Akhtar, a young journalist who has devoted her entire life to carve out a niche for herself in the male-dominated world, tries to motivate, instigate, inspire other girls of her own community, who had been holed up in the inner recesses, to take up cudgels against the narrow-mindedness of the outside world and seize the reins of their life in their own hands. She dares to toll the bell against the mindset that lay crushed for centuries, but her own life gets mired in controversy and she finds herself sinking in the same quagmire in her journey towards self-realization.

The novel also very poignantly describes the pitiable plight of Nazma who is wedded to her own cousin brother at a tender age of 15, when she does not even know what marriage entails. In her naivety she mistakenly comes to regard the marital rape as her husband's love for her, to which she is subjected every night and is left badly battered, both physically and psychologically.

The all-protective upbringing accorded to this young girl, has turned her into a marionette who dances to the whims and fancies of the males in her life. She ends up being pushed into complete oblivion and is rendered virtually invisible. She gets tossed from one *rehnuma* to the other, none of whom are in the least inclined to peep into her heart and see what lay beneath.

Who are these *rehnumas*?

Rehnumas are the all-knowing all-powerful patriarchs whose word is a kind of unwritten law which needs to be adhered to by all the family members. More often than not, this very patronage of theirs becomes counterproductive owing to their larger-than-life egos that turn them myopic and parochial. They fail to empathize with the plight of their protegees.

Oh, These Rehnumas! brings out poignantly the travails faced by scores of women like Taha and Nazma to the center-stage.

Though it is a theme that has been oft written about, but what grips is the deft writing style and the effortless ease of the nimble narrative which keeps the reader glued.

Many a times, the small vignettes thrown in-between reveal the inner recesses of female psyche so adroitly that it gives us goosebumps. The intermingling of Hindustani and Urdu *zubaan* lends an authentic flavor of the community about whom it is written.

The wonderfully nuanced and relatable characters who are caught in a *cul-de-sac,* induce us to shed our veneer of detachment and identify with their dilemmas and predicaments. It is no wonder that there has been one Doctorate and two M.Phil. dissertations undertaken on this novel.

Tasneem Khan has been shortisted for the *Bhartiya Jnanpith* Award in the *Navlekan* category for the year 2016 for her debut novel, ***Ae Mere Rehnuma*** which inspired me to pick it up in the very first place. Even before I finished reading it, I had made a resolve to translate it into English so as to pave way for it to reach a much wider audience.

I faced several challenges during the course of my translation, I got stalled a number of times to find the right equivalents. The foremost of them all was to find a word that could convey the essence of the title word, *'rehnuma'*. Patron, leader, custodian, guardian angel, patriarch, were the choices in front of me, but none of them could express the core connotation behind it. The closest that I could find was 'godfather', someone who protects and guides and has the well-being of his protegees in mind. He is also someone who is used to having his own way, someone who doesn't like his path to be crossed. But as I bounced it off with my friends and well-wishers, the association with 'godfather' was more with mafia don, all due credits to Mario Puzo's legendry novel by the same name. And finally, I settled for *Rehnuma*, which has no equally powerful parallel in English language. To facilitate the flow of the narrative, I have added small footnotes wherever required.

Here I would like take the opportunity to thank Tasneem Khan, for having readily consented for me to undertake this translation. I would also like to express my heartfelt gratitude to my friend and spouse, Arvind Elhance, without whose encouragement and constant support, the present work would have been difficult.

— *Jyotika Elhance*

Oh, These Rehnumas!

The packed house reverberated with a loud applause. It was the annual function of the College for Women and on the stage were present many celebrities. The entire college was abuzz with their presence. The students were unable to conceal their excitement at seeing the women they idolized in front of them. They were all eagerly waiting for the function to be over so that they could click selfies with them and post them on the Facebook and garner innumerable 'likes'. Presently their entire attention was captured by their success stories. It appeared as if they were keenly looking forward to following in their foot-steps. There were festivities everywhere. It wasn't just the College Annual Day; it was the Women's Day as well. Madam Chief Minister had just finished addressing the students and now it was the turn of the other guest speakers. The auditorium once again echoed with a loud applause when Mrs. Jain, the Chair-person, Women's Commission began to address the students.

A little later, when Taha took a couple of steps towards the mic, the applause grew to a deafening pitch. The students became extremely excited and started cheering her loudly. They were dying to hear her speak. Taha waved at the audience and moved ahead with winsome smile and oodles of self-confidence. She wore a light pink colored salwar-suit and carried her dupatta in her very own characteristic style that added charm to her otherwise somber appearance. Her hair was left open just like her thoughts. Every step that she took oozed of self-assurance and poise. This extremely liberal-minded and confident woman had a huge fan following. The fully packed auditorium resounded with loud cheers. But when she took the mic in her hand to speak, there was pin-drop silence. Such was her craze in the audience. Nobody wanted to miss even a single word of hers. The audience, especially the girls and young women, present there were awestruck by the magic of her voice. She began,

'This is your life! Live it as you want to live. Dream big. Put your heart and soul into realizing your dreams. Let no man stop you. There'd be many people who'd try to stall your progress and they'd be from those who are very close to you. Do not let them sabotage your life. Ignore them and concentrate only on achieving your dreams. The patriarchal mind-set would forever be putting obstacles in your path. They would never want you to become independent. They would never want you to succeed in life. For if you do, they would feel their control slipping away from their hands. You are not their property. You are not under their patronage'.

She continued further, 'Control your lives. Take the reins of your life in your own hands. Empower your own selves. And the first step towards it is financial freedom. Take up a job and become someone. Be financially independent. A lot of problems would automatically get taken care of. Then there would neither be the shackles of patriarchy nor its violence. You would never again be oppressed by the narrow-minded orthodoxy. Women have been at the receiving end of all the atrocities because they have been kept financially weak and dependent on men folk. Times have changed. Women are no longer afraid now.'

'Taha…Taha…Taha…', reverberated everywhere.

Taha was their role model, their Hero! She had carved out a niche for herself in this male-dominated society. She had the gift of weaving magic with words that made the crowd go ecstatic. She had moved her audience to such fervor that without giving much thought, many of them avowed to emulate her and take control of their own lives. They asserted that they wouldn't allow anyone to interfere in their lives and would tackle firmly with anyone and everyone who tried to stall their progress. There were some others too in the auditorium who wanted to become reporters like her.

'*Wah*, Taha *baji*! You were simply amazing. Everything went off seamlessly. You breathed so much life in the entire program. There was appreciation from both sides, the management as well as the client. The credit for it all goes to you, *baji*. Thank you so much,' I said expressing my admiration for her as we sat down together for refreshments.

'Please Anam, at least you don't say such things. They sound good in speeches only. You are very well aware of how things actually stand for me', dropping her gaze Taha murmured. Her down-cast eyes spoke volumes.

They both sat there quietly without uttering a word more.

'When are we meeting like friends again? There are so many things that I wanted to share with you…,' Taha tried to change the topic and the silence was broken.

'Soon, let's meet soon. Let's meet at our old favorite coffee shop.'

'Sure…'

On that note we both parted ways.

I left for office to hand over the details of the Annual Day program.

'Come Anam, come in. I heard that the program was a big hit'. My boss welcomed me as I stepped into the office.

'Yes, Sir. It was indeed. Here are all the details.'

'Well done!' Anam, Congratulations. Our P. R. Agency needs more people like you.'

'Thank You, Sir', I smiled happily and looked at my watch, "Sir, it's six o'clock. If you allow me, I'd like to go home.'

'This is what I don't like about you women. Always in a rush to go back home. You are professionals but you don't behave like one. And then you complain that you don't get as much standing and raises as menfolk do.' The boss remarked a trifle callously, signaling me to leave for the day.

I felt quite dejected by his snide comment. The elation of having accomplished the program successfully, vanished into thin air and I left the office without saying a word.

The small verandah outside the house has always been my favorite place. My husband and I would sit there with our cup of coffee and relax in the evening after reaching home.

We didn't have a garden nor was there much greenery around but this had become a place where we could un-wind and relax. There was a big wall that separated it from the main road outside. Although we could not see the view of the outer area, but it provided privacy as well as security from unwanted visitors and burglars. I could gaze at the skies for hours on end and watch the twilight glow of the setting sun and the star and moon studded skies from here. Seeing the glow-worms dancing was enough to fill me with happiness.

I used to find it calming to sit amidst these potted plants. For here I had buried the memories of the village where I had grown up as a child. Although there were no huge verandahs and sprawling gardens with cool breeze blowing through them, but this small corner provided me with the much-needed succor.

The paucity of place only allowed us the liberty of keeping just 8 to10 pots wherein we grew jasmine, raat-rani and money-plant. Jasmine and raat-rani were my preferred plants whereas Alim and Mahira liked the money-plant more. My daughter loved plucking its leaves and folding them like *paan* and offer it to us. This was her game. Seeing his favorite leaves plucked in this manner used to make my husband mad. He used to feel as if someone was plucking his heart out and he would very often end up scolding her.

The soft breeze found some respite from the hot afternoon sun and had begun to cool down slightly. And the fluttering leaves of money-plant that lay strewn on the ground, began to transport me to a different world altogether wherein I felt that life wasn't as harsh. My husband and I usually sit in this verandah and chat about the day's happenings over our cup of coffee. Today also he was sitting on the chair next to me and our six-year-old daughter was busy playing with her toys nearby.

'You had ordered some household things in the morning?' asked my husband.

'Yes, I had left the list on top of the almirah. Wasn't it there?'

'Yes, it was...but only the list.'

I understood what he was hinting at, but kept quiet.

'You know how expensive things have become.'

'You buy five items and a thousand-rupee note just vanishes. And you know it's the month-end and my tuitions also are not doing too well.'

After a grueling day at office, this kind of snide comment from my husband annoyed me.

'Why? Isn't it the month-end for me too? It's not as if I got my salary only yesterday', I retorted back.

'So, your money is for saving and mine is for indulging in frivolous luxuries?' my husband shouted back. 'Why do you go to work if you can't spend on household things?'

'Whatever I get, I spend it on the house only. What am I left with? Whatever savings I make are also in your name. You too earn so much. Where does your money go?' I countered.

'If it is in my name, why are you so upset? Don't I have any right on your money? Besides, am I running away with your savings? It will be used for the three of us only,' he said indignantly.

I kept quiet.

'What I do with the money and what I don't is none of your business. I neither think it necessary to share the information with you nor do I think you have the right to know,' he further added authoritatively.

'I didn't mean that. I also need some money for myself. But you make me spend on everything.' I said defensively.

I felt very hurt and alone.

'You are neither able to take care of the house properly nor are able to bring up our daughter well. And to top it all, you throw your weight around because you are earning. Go and hand over your resignation letter tomorrow. You have enough and more on your hand. Sit at home. You don't need to go out and do a job', thundered Alim.

He knew very well that this threat of his was my biggest weakness. I would not be able to continue with my job at the cost of his anger. This is exactly what we've been taught right from our childhood days. It had been drilled into us that relations come first and especially that of a husband. The façade of relationship has to be maintained even if it means losing your own identity. This has been engrained so deeply into our minds that even if we want, we would never be able to rid ourselves of it. There were tears in her eyes.

'Mumma, Mumma...' Mahira was shouting for her.

'Mumma, what should I become when I grow up?' she asked. She would ask the same question every day.

'You become whatever you want to become', I replied patting her on the cheeks.

'My daughter's going to become an astronaut and go to moon', Alim said taking Mahira in his lap.

'No Papa, I'm going to become police. I'll beat anyone who fights.'

The innocuous remark from the child eased off the bitterness between the sparring couple and made them smile. The evening gradually blended into night and the sweet fragrance of jasmine and raat-rani flowers engulfed them in its fold and lightened their mood.

Wiping the perspiration, I came out of the kitchen and stood directly under the fan. It was nine forty-five by the clock that was hanging on the front wall.

'It's still not ten and it is so hot already.'

It was the same routine every day. I'd first finish all the kitchen work and then whatever time that was left with, I would tidy up the house, often wondering whether the clock was moving with me or I was moving with the clock. Alim would leave for his college at seven o'clock. Being a Lecturer of a private college was quite cool. He used to work from seven to twelve and then was free to come home and relax. In the afternoons, he would take some tuition. But for women-folk it's a different story. The word 'relax' is not meant for them. It doesn't exist in their dictionary. They keep shuttling tirelessly between home and office. In my own heart of hearts, I used to envy Alim.

'Mumma, Mumma...I know what I'll become', Mahira's voice jolted me out of my thoughts.

She placed a colored page of a newspaper in my lap.

'Look here, it's Taha Aunty'.

That was yesterday's program that was printed in the newspaper.

'Mumma I'll become Taha Aunty when I grow up. Then my pictures also would come in the newspapers. And when my friend, Muniya sees them she'll be surprised', waving her arms Mahira said innocently.

I didn't like Mahira disturbing me in the midst of work, but I just smiled to please her and said, 'Okay dear'.

Saying this I got busy in other chores. 'Oh, if I'm not able to make it for the 12 o'clock meeting, there'll be chaos in office. I'll have to face the Manager's ire and besides that, scores of warnings too. And this woman hasn't arrived as yet.'

Mahira's clothes lay strewn all over. Why can't Alim pick them up and keep them at the right place. He himself doesn't put his own clothes on hanger, instead leaves them on the floor as if he'd never wear them again.

Oh, the bed also hasn't been made!

It just takes five minutes to do that but he does not do even that much. I only have to keep the house in order. I only have to go out and earn and also take care of all the household responsibilities. I can't even expect him to share the burden with me. Why? Because he's a man and men don't work in the house. They only work outside the house to earn money. I was muttering to myself when I heard the gate open. Heaving a long sigh of relief, I called out loudly,

'Is this the time to come to work? It has become a daily habit. You come late every day and have some or the other excuse ready...I've asked you a thousand times to come by 9:30 so that I'm also able to reach office in time,' in a single breath I transferred all my anger and frustration on to her. It meant that I was tired and over-worked too.

As usual there was no response from the other side. She quietly began with her routine household chores, swept the terrace, staircase...

Today also she did not say anything to my outburst. I left the remaining work on her and went for my bath. When I was standing in front of the mirror, I happened to see Shyama Di's face. It looked somewhat different. Her usual smile too was missing as our eyes met across the dressing mirror. She seemed to be lost somewhere.

'What happened Shyama Didi? You are looking sad today.' I turned towards her.

She looked at me for a moment and then dropped her gaze.

Oh my God! All these black and blue marks on your face! 'What's that? Are you unwell?'

She just shook her head without uttering a word.

'No, there is something wrong. Tell me what happened?' I insisted.

'There is nothing unusual in this. If your own fate has tied you to such a man, what else can happen?', Shyama Didi replied very softly.

'That means today again you've been beaten up. I have told you so many times that if he comes home drunk and beats you up, you also beat him back. You'll see how quickly he'll give up this nasty habit of his.'

'Where would I go after beating him up, *bhabhi*. I'll have to be staying with him only. I have daughters who have to be married off. What would people say?'

She continued further, 'And whenever a house breaks up, it's always woman who is held responsible. Men always go scot-free. Do they ever get blamed? If I hadn't been worried about this blame game and the social stigma attached with it, I would have left him years ago.'

Her arguments left me speechless. Why should the onus of buying peace always fall upon a woman alone? Why should she be the one to make all the sacrifices? I found myself entangled in Shyama Didi's problems. The entire responsibility of bringing up her five children, their school fees, kitchen and other expenses rested on her shoulders. Her husband never contributed to it at all. In fact, it was the other way round. He too lived off her. Despite all this, she remained subservient to him. Her life was badly trapped under the societal pressures.

Shyama Didi herself was tall and well-built with dusky complexion. She had long thick black hair which she always kept well-oiled and tightly braided. She used to live in a village nearby and was the eldest of three sisters. They did not have any brother and that is why their father had become old much before his time working single-handedly in the fields for, he had the task of seeing his daughters married off somehow.

Shyama Didi's in-law's house was in the town but she stayed in a small *kuchcha-pacca* house behind our colony. It was a very small room with verandah in which she lived with her two sons and three daughters. They had another small room upstairs too in which her sister in-law used to stay with her family. And in a small shack in the corner of the verandah stayed her mother in-law who would invariably be heard calling her out as 'karamjali' i.e., an ill-fated woman. Her father in-law had passed away years ago. The house would be not more than fifty square yards. It wasn't even enough for one family leave alone three families that were staying there instead.

And to top it all, they also had a cow that used to be tied in the courtyard that was so small that the poor animal could either stand or sit. There was no place for it to move at all. It kept mooing endlessly trying to ward off the flies. The inmates of the house could not move in or out of the house without brushing against the cow. And at times on the ground of this very courtyard, Shyama Didi could be spotted lying down, tending to her wounds and bruises.

'I'm through with my work *bhabhi*, I'm leaving.' Shyama Didi's voice broke my reverie.

'Alright, now go home and take some rest. And what I would suggest, leave your work so that your husband also realizes his own responsibility and gets into the habit of earning a living.'

In response Shyama gave a faint smile and left.

It was eleven o'clock by the time I reached office after dropping Mahira at her day-boarding school. I dashed across the parking lot to my office as I remembered about the meeting with the Manager. Leaving my purse at the desk, I entered the room. The meeting had already started. There was no new agenda to be discussed. The Manager was as usual blowing his own trumpet, singing praises about his own achievements and finding faults with everyone's work.

In these meetings, I deliberately used to choose a seat behind a colleague so that the Manager could only see my face and not the hands. That way I could check my Facebook and WhatsApp and still be part of the meeting. It wasn't that I was a bad employee who was hoodwinking her employer when he was discussing some important issues. Everyone present there were just killing time wanting the inane meeting to get over. Vimleshji shared a WhatsApp post on the group just then and people were taking turns to steal a look into their mobile phones. He had written,

"Managed to save four days from life somehow,

Two got spent on Facebook, two on Boss's rebuke."

I was about to burst into laughter but managed to suppress it in the nick of time. And in the bargain my face turned deep red.

The Manager's voice droned drearily on the other side, 'It seems I've gathered a whole army of useless people. You people aren't able to complete your own commitments on time and it is I who am left facing the brunt of all the complaints from clients. Look at me, I give twelve to thirteen hours to this office'

The Manager's tone became harsher. His employees were finding it extremely difficult to contain their laughter. When Sharmaji found the situation getting out of hand, he excused himself and rushed out of the hall. As soon as he left, the boss also realized that out of the precious twelve to thirteen hours of his time that he gives to his office-work daily, he had needlessly spent a good hour and a half raising his blood pressure. He quickly concluded the meeting by saying, 'so, the meeting is over.'

Without wasting a single second, everybody dashed out of the hall as if they had suddenly developed severe stomach cramps and were in urgent need to use the wash-room. They came out and accosted Vimlesh for putting them in such a soup. A little later, they all proceeded towards their desks to complete the tasks assigned to them.

Of all days, today the weather had become very pleasant. It was afternoon and there was a slight drizzle. The winters were almost over and the raindrops brought in a slight chill. The four of us stepped out of the office and came to the canteen for lunch. This was the 'us-time' which we stole for ourselves from our otherwise busy office schedule and gossiped with no holds barred. We cherished this togetherness as it gave us a brief respite from the deafening crematorium-like silence of the office environment. And to add spice to our chats our mother in-laws, husbands and bosses came in very handy. No conversation was complete without bringing them into it.

'Hahaha…ha...ha', the canteen resounded with everyone's laughter.

It meant that it was someone's turn to get ragged.

And today I happened to be that person.

'Look at this great woman. Her name is Anam. Today she has taught her maid to draw daggers against her own husband…against the social system'. Manjulata stood up and began her tirade in a grand manner.

'Now why are you sitting there with a glum face? When you don't have guts enough to confront your own husband, how can you preach others?' taunted Seema.

'But my husband doesn't come home drunk and beat me, so why should I confront him?' I retorted angrily.

'That's enough. You don't have to keep up appearances before us. We all know the reality, so stop playing the innocent,' Seema wasn't the one to get cowed down easily.

My mood got spoilt and the dish in front of me tasted like saw-dust.

'Alright, so tell me what I should have said?'

"Oh woman! Poor woman!

How sad is the plight of thy existence!

Thy hands hold the Marriage certificate

And eyes the weight of tears unshed !!"

Manju began the couplet and the other three completed it.

Soma said, 'Had I been in your place, I would have done exactly the same thing. Our situation is not very different from hers. We are all in the same boat wherein we have to keep up the social pretenses of this ostensibly civilized world of ours.'

'Yes, I too have been beaten umpteen number of times by that rascal of a husband of mine, but never once did you ask me to revolt against him like this', chipped in Manju revealing her own wretched status at home in her usual jovial manner.

'Oh, I thought your husband's name was *Parmeshwar* and you are calling him rascal. Oh God! Please forgive her.' Looking towards the sky Soma joined her palms in prayer.

'Oh, your husband is also *Parmeshwar* and mine also is *Parmeshwar*. In fact, every woman's husband is a *Parmeshwar*. This is what we have been taught right from our childhood days', winked Seema and extended the jest a little further.

'Given a chance I'd like to throw my husband, your husband, her husband, maid's husband, in fact, all the husbands of this world in a deep and blind well', spat Manjulata passionately and all the friends burst out laughing. And with it all their pent-up bitterness vanished into thin air. The full-hearted laughter and the light drizzle elevated their moods and they felt extremely light.

'I feel it's Taha Akhtar's speech that has driven her insane that she's contemplating revolt against the system. Dear Madam, get a hold on yourself. Every woman cannot be as fortunate as Taha. She is strong both personally and professionally. Haven't you seen Taha and her husband strolling together hand in hand? He doesn't seem to have any problem with her friends circle also. He enjoys joking and laughing with them equally.' Soma's mind was working overtime.

'No friends, I think now you are digressing from the topic. Let's get back to work as lunch time is over'. I stood up from my chair and everyone followed suit.

'Yes dear, I really envy Taha. Every now and then she's in news, making headlines. I can bet that unless and until a middle-class woman gets support from her husband, she cannot achieve such powerful position.' Seema also agreed with Soma's views.

'Why are you so quiet, Anam? She's your close friend, isn't she…?' Soma asked.

Cutting her in mid-sentence I said, 'Oh forget all this nonsense. I have to go on an assignment and I'm getting late.'

As they were coming out of the canteen, they saw Nisha waving goodbye to someone at the main gate.

'Here comes Miss Aids shop'.

'That's not right, Manju. I don't like this derogatory language of yours towards women.'

'Why? It's not I alone who says that. The entire office knows it pretty well that she's staying in a live-in relationship with her boyfriend. Neither does she marry him nor allows him to marry anyone else.'

'So how does it matter to you? It's her life, let her do what she wants.'

'Let her do it? I'm not stopping her. But whatever is not socially acceptable would be called wrong only.'

'It's pointless to argue with you.'

'What's there to argue in this? If she loves him then why doesn't she marry him?'

All three of them ignored Manju's comment and walked towards their office.

Today was another dull and dreary morning. The same routine work, the same tiredness nothing new. And to top it all, today again Shyama Didi was late. She'd have the same old excuse: husband beat her up and was asking for money and what not! Many a time, I feel that women unnecessarily paint their husbands worse than they really are in order to gain sympathy. Look at Manisha Ma'am, she keeps crying all day and is hardly able to work but the boss also doesn't say anything to her.

'When would Alim ever learn to keep things in place?' picking and folding the newspaper I muttered. I felt frustrated. As I was about to put it on the table my eyes fell on a familiar face.

'Oh, who could that be? The face looks so familiar,' I scanned the paper a little more closely. 'This looks like Taha *Baji*!'

'Oh yes! This is Taha *Baji* for sure!' The newspaper report says she is no more.

'Taha Akhtar, well-known journalist passed away on Wednesday. The funeral procession would be at 2 o' clock on Thursday afternoon after the Zuhr *namaz*. May Allah give her soul a place in heaven. Amen. Husband: Zeeshan Ali & Family. Address: C-134, Pratap Nagar, Jaipur.'

I was completely dumb-struck. My eyes were glued to the obituary. I read it over and over again. My worst fears had come true. For months I had a lurking fear of this kind of an eventuality. But now that it was staring at me, I found it difficult to believe. Taha, who had always been a strong and independent woman, who had charted the course of her own destiny and achieved unprecedented success, today lay defeated at the hands of her own fate or was it by her own people!

My reverie was broken by the phone ring. Wiping the tears off my cheeks I picked up. It was Sheeba on the other side.

'Anam *Baji*, did you get the news? I can't believe that Taha *Baji* is no more. I got to know just now only. You are coming for the cremation, aren't you?' she blurted in one breath.

I just said 'Yes' and cut the phone. I didn't have any more words than this. My eyes were fixed on her photograph. Why do women who fight for their rights and dreams always get such a raw deal from life? Why do their own near and dear ones leave no stone unturned to defeat them? Outwardly, these so-called successful women ooze confidences, but inwardly they have been sucked dry ...bereft of all love, affection and trust. They stand all alone.

I felt the pain and frustration of her life gradually seeping into me.

The women who cross the threshold of their homes in order to fulfill their dreams rarely find solace in their deaths too. This was the message that Taha's obituary seemed to spell out loud and clear.

I called up my office to inform them that I'd be on leave. The Manager, as usual got a little upset and said, 'If you continue on like this, then the day is not far when you'd make me close down my P.R. agency.'

I mumbled a reply under my breath and put the phone down.

Pratap Nagar, where *Baji* used to stay, was on the outskirts of the town. But in a fast-growing metro city like Jaipur, 25 kms wasn't considered much of a distance. But reaching there by scooty, it was indeed. With a heavy heart I set for her house.

It was just a couple of days back that I had visited her house with my husband and daughter. She had been quite insistent and had invited us over for dinner to celebrate her younger son's *nashra.* Munaf had completed his first reading of the entire Quran.

Even if I had not visited her house earlier, it wouldn't have been difficult for me or for any stranger for that matter to locate her residence as the crowd was spilling over on the outer lanes. It seemed the entire town had gathered there to pay their obeisance to her. I parked my scooty in a nearby plot where several other cars were also parked and headed towards her house.

The area wasn't very thickly populated. There were many plots that were still lying vacant. On one side there was a huge park around which there were about ten-twelve sprawling bungalows. One of them belonged to Taha *Baji*. She had been staying there for the past ten years approximately. Earlier, she used to stay in the main-town with her in-laws. When her father bought a house in this area to escape the claustrophobic atmosphere of the city, Taha also did the same. Since she was a working woman, she wanted to stay close to her parents so that they could take care of her children when she was away.

She used to call it her dream-house.

Lost in these thoughts, I reached her house and found hundreds of men and women standing there with their heads covered. Despite the massive gathering of friends and family, there was pin-drop silence. The room, the veranda, the entire place was packed to the brim. Every inch of space was full. Wanting to take one last look at her, I cut across the crowd and entered the central hall. It was here that she used to play host to so many of her friends.

On one side lay Taha's coffin enveloped by the fragrance emanating from the incense-sticks that were put there. The low wailing sounds of the mourners seemed to dampen the aroma. There were tears in every eye and gloom on every face. The *Maulana* along with both of her brothers were reciting *Surah Al Baqarah*.

She lay there, all covered in her shroud, looking very pure and pristine. Although there were some dark circles below her eyes but even that could not diminish the glow on her face. Her hair, which she always kept open in her usual style, were covered under the shroud.

It seemed Taha *Baji* had finally decided to step down from the busy roller-coaster life of hers and call it complete quits. Today no bawling, no bellowing, no sobs, no sniffles seem to reach her. Her deep-rooted quest for eternal peace has at last been fulfilled after years of endless suffering. Everyone knew how gritty she was. They knew that she would not rest till she accomplished what she wanted.

'Oh, my darling daughter, my life! Why didn't Allah take my life and spare yours! Hey almighty, what was lacking in my prayers that you took away my child from me? You could've taken pity on her poor children at least.'

Then came a piercing shriek and Taha's Ammi passed out. Her

relatives immediately came forward to help. They sprinkled some water on her face, she wavered in and out of her consciousness, but remained largely unaware of her surrounding and kept muttering under her breath.

Taha's sister also couldn't look after her mother, for the grief had shattered her too. Her senses had gone numb. Firstly, the grief of passing away of her elder sister and secondly the heart-wrenching plight of her two nephews who had lost their mother at such a tender age. Every soul present there was heartbroken.

Ten-year-old Umar and eight-year-old Munaf both sat quietly in one corner of the room looking lost. Umar, however seemed to have some inkling of what had befallen them but young Munaf was completely unaware of the fact that he had been rendered orphan (if the father passes away, mother fills in his absence, but when mother dies, father cannot take her place, so I would call them orphans only).

The hall was full of mourning women. I spotted Sheeba sitting in one corner. She signaled me to come over, but I decided otherwise and found a place near the feet of *Baji's* mortal remains. I sat there and rested my head against the wall.

Taha *Baji*, and I were like bosom pals, very attached to each other. We shared so many secrets together. She was like my elder sister, my close friend. Although we were seven or eight years apart, but we got along well. Our friendship was thicker than that of most of the same age friends. We were close confidants and were genuinely concerned about each other's well-being.

She was my ideal whom I wanted to emulate. She inspired me by her exemplary ways. Never did she succumb to the social pressures, always lived life on her own terms. It wasn't my daughter, Mahira alone who wanted to be like her, I too wanted to follow in her footsteps.

And today, she lay before us lifeless. What does it all entail? Does it mean that one day I too would be broken down?

People used to be envious of Taha *Baji* for she had successfully carved out a niche for herself in this society that was dominated largely by menfolk. What they couldn't see was that how difficult it was to be a woman in this patriarchal world. To achieve their rightful place in the society, to claim their own space and to forge their own identity wasn't a cakewalk.

This was exactly what Taha *Baji* had done. She had the audacity to challenge the male order. Everyone saw her gradually inching towards success, but no one saw the wounds that she had incurred in the bargain. She always presented a brave front before people. She didn't want them to see her battered inner-self, for if they did, the vast majority of women, who had dared to dream of freedom, would get disheartened and retrace their steps back into the age-old shackles of orthodoxy. She kept up the pretense in order to inspire the young girls to leave their claustrophobic lives behind and step into a world where a completely new life awaited them.

'Taha…Tahu, where are you, my darling? Hashim Miya called his dear daughter as he entered the house.

They had a very small ancestral house that stood right at the center of the Ghatgate market. During his father's time, the house was quite big, but afterwards when the property was divided amongst four brothers, they had barely 80-85 sq. yards piece. Hashim Miya had constructed two small rooms and a small kitchen. There was one room upstairs too which was normally used whenever they had guests. They hadn't covered the courtyard although an extra room would have come in handy, but he didn't want the place to be dark and dinghy as was the case with so many of the city houses that he had seen.

As he removed his leather shoes to put them in the shoe-rack outside, Taha came running out and jumped on his shoulders.

'Oh, Oh, who is there on my back….?' Pretending to play a guessing game, he hugged his daughter tightly and stood up. Taha closed his eyes with her small palms beaming happily. He came inside and put her down on the sofa, then feigning surprise he exclaimed, 'Oh, I see, isn't this my very own darling daughter!'

And Taha gave a gurgling laughter and snatched the bag from his hands.

'Today again, you've bought rasagullas and chocolates. This way you'd spoil her habit and her teeth too. Taha's mother, Shahida Begum chided him indulgently yet affectionately and took the bag from Taha. Taha followed her mother into the kitchen.

This was their everyday exchange. Shahida Begum would pretend to be angry but would lovingly put the sweets in a small bowl and give it to her daughter. The daughter would happily sit in her father's lap and spend hours eating them.

Relaxing on a high bed with a big round pillow under her arm, Hashim Miya's mother also would lovingly watch this inter-play of affection between the father-daughter duo, but she would also throw in a word of caution saying, 'Hashim, it's not right to be so attached with daughters….'. And she would feel her own words echoing back to her in a distance. Hashim Miya's only response was an indulgent smile.

Taha's birth brought a lot of good fortune for Hashim Miya. After she was born, his life had taken an upward swing, bringing him joy and contentment aplenty. He, who had been unemployed for so long, got the government job that he had long cherished. Hashim Miya always wanted his second child to be a girl only and when his dream came true, he showered all his love on her.

Even before she was born, Hashim always used to say to his wife, 'Every house should have a daughter. Girls bring in so much sunshine and sparkle into the house with their incessant prattle that the house comes alive. Their very presence and innocuous laughter fill the house with new life'

Shahida Begum would bashfully ask, 'What would happen if the second child also is a boy…then...?'

At this he would pout lovingly to show that he was upset.

One day, he surprised his wife when he bought a small baby frock, a little doll and a pair of small booties but ended up annoying his mother hugely. She scolded him, 'Have you lost your mind Hashim? This is not a good omen! Night and day, I'm only praying for the second child to be a boy and you are foolishly asking for a daughter. I want the second one also to be a boy. If you want a daughter, then you can have the third one. If Allah grants me my wish, I'd go to *durgah* and offer a floral tribute.'

'Amma, you are still caught in old times. Today both are equal. There is no difference between a boy and a girl,' Hashim Miya retorted back.

'I know that, but I'll still say two brothers are better than one. After that it doesn't matter whether it's a boy or a girl. Both the brothers would be there to take care of their sister,' replied Amma.

'Why would they take care of her? She'd look after herself when she grows up. Why would she be dependent on her brothers?'

At this Amma got irritated and said, 'You and your foolish ideas! Reserve them for your office and office colleagues. Don't give me that jargon.'

She continued, 'It's the sons who carry forward the legacy. They are the ones who bring in name and fame for the family. Whereas the daughters would leave behind everything and go to their respective homes one day.'

'It was probably this very mindset of yours that did not allow Nazma to attend school. If you had got her educated also, like you did with her brothers, then probably she wouldn't have had to depend on her husband for each new paisa.'

Hashim Miya's brusque remark reopened the wounds of yester years and Amma's tone softened immediately.

She said, 'How does it matter? All her four brothers are there to fulfill her each and every need, isn't it?' After a long pause she added further, 'She's able to manage her household with the money that all of you give to her. I don't know what would have happened if you weren't there? Her plight would have been really pitiable.'

Amma looked away trying hard to hide her inner turmoil.

Her voice reflected a sense of misplaced pride. The manner in which it faltered and crackled down, made it amply clear that somewhere deep down she still felt guilty for not having got her daughter educated as well as she did her sons. Despite the passage of time, the pain still rankled and prevented her from sharing it with her children. But the crisscrossing of expressions on her old freckled face revealed it all.

Hashim Miya cursed himself for having upset his mother unnecessarily. It had happened so long back. Why did he have to rake it up again? He knew fully well that what had been done cannot be undone now? Besides, Amma was now too old to be taunted about these things any longer.

Vexed with himself, he immediately tried to change the topic and assuage the situation but Amma had sealed her lips. She probably wanted to be left alone.

Hashim Miya got up and went into the balcony. His sister's face flashed before his eyes and he began to miss her very much. Apart from helping out with some money once in a while, he wasn't able to do much for her. Money took care of her financial needs but it wasn't enough to make her life better.

Nazma was the youngest of all the brothers. She was the darling of the house. They used to lovingly call her 'Gudiya'. She only studied till fifth standard and after that was put to household tasks as that was considered to be her present as well as future too.

Abba said, 'Gudiya is getting older and should better stay indoors. It isn't good for her to venture outside. And since she is a girl, she wouldn't have to go out to earn a livelihood. Then where is the need to send her to school? Besides, we have no desire to live off her money.' He further said, 'And how would we be able to find a right match for her if she becomes over qualified? The groom and his family are more interested in a domesticated bride who is docile and uneducated.'

That was what Abba used to believe and as a result Gudiya was never allowed to go out at all. The only life that she had been allowed to live, was the one that was limited within the four walls of the house.

She too wanted to go to school to study further like her brothers. When that didn't happen, she started picking up their books to read. Kareem, her elder brother understood her keenness and wanted to request Abba to allow her to attend school, but the day he advocated her case, all hell broke loose.

Abba put his foot down authoritatively and bellowed, 'Till I'm alive, it's my orders that would be followed in this household and in your lives as well. All five of you are my children. Whatever I do, I do it for the good of you all. If I'm not allowing Gudiya to go to school, it's for her benefit only. I don't want her to study any further.'

'You cannot hold her back in this manner. If you don't want to step out of the constrictive well, it's your wish. But Gudiya is today's girl. You cannot give her a life entangled in orthodoxy.' Kareem's young blood was on the boil in front of his father.

'Now I really feel that I've made a big mistake by educating you all. The elders have rightly said that these schools and colleges only lead the young astray.'

His face was red with rage as he put forth his warped logic before him. And the skin at the center of his forehead, where it touched the ground while offering the *Namaz*, began to seethe in anger.

Gudiya stood crest-fallen behind the doors, sheepishly watching the changing colors on her father's face. Her father was a powerful man with an impressive personality. He was tall, fair and a broad-shouldered man, who always used to be dressed in either grey or black salwar-kameez. Despite his advanced age, the hair on his head and beard were still thick and black. The glow on his face could give any young man a run for his money. And the grey mark of *namaz* on his forehead added a touch of gravity to his striking persona.

Gudiya understood that it was futile to argue with him. Come what may, her father would stand his ground firmly. So, without a whimper of protest, she very quietly doused acid on her dreams so that not a single trace is left behind. She buried them forever.

With the passage of time, this young girl turned into a grave and responsible adult at a very tender age. She threw herself completely into household chores and mastered the art of coking. Biryani, korma, chicken kababs whatever she cooked, it used to be delicious. So much so that from then onwards her mother too stopped going into the kitchen as Gudiya was able to handle everything so well.

She wouldn't have been more than fifteen years old when she was betrothed to her cousin brother. Abba came home one day and broke this good news; Ammi was very pleased. She immediately kissed Gudiya's forehead to ward off any evil-eye. Her daughter would soon become a bride and go to her marital house. And she would be relieved of all her responsibilities and obligations towards her.

When her elder brother came to know about this in the evening, he immediately went and confronted his father, 'Why are you in such a tearing hurry to get her married off? Let's wait for the right match.'

Abba snapped back, 'Where is the need to wait further? She'd be going to my elder brother's house only. Won't she be happy there?'

'Abba, you know Wasim, what a wastrel he is? He hasn't been able to clear his tenth standard also. Neither does he earn anything. You still want to marry your daughter to him?'

'What do you mean? Should I let go off such a good match simply because he's not earning right now? He's also part of our family. He's my elder brother's son. How can we call him a wastrel? And Gudiya isn't going to an unknown house. She'd remain before our eyes even after her marriage. And, God forbid, even if any unfortunate situation does arise, we'd be all there to help them out.'

Abba tried to persuade his son, but it angered him further.

'Abba, let's wait for a couple of more years. Maybe we'd be able to find a better match for her. And anyways, isn't she also under-age right now,' the son tried his best to reason out with his father.

'You don't teach me "laws". According to me, this is absolutely the right age for a girl to marry.'

'Abba, you don't have to hide behind the *sharia law* every time. You need to be more pragmatic, times have changed,' Kareem retorted edgily.

Abba also lost his cool and shouted back at him, 'Now you people would teach me what's right and what's wrong? I have given my word to my brother. Gudiya is getting married on *Eid* and that is final. If you want, you can be part of the festivities, otherwise you can stay away.'

He left no room for any further debate.

Standing behind the doors, Gudiya desperately prayed for the argument to end. She was too young to understand the gravity of the situation. And how could she understand anything? Until now she had been blindly treading the path chosen by her father, doing things that were told to her, like an automaton. She had got so used to following instructions that if she were asked to live one day according to her own wishes, she'd feel lost. She had been turned into a puppet-a puppet whose strings were controlled by her father's hands.

Abba was her guardian angel, her god, her *rehnuma*, she was completely devoted to him. In other words, it wouldn't be wrong to say that this right to her own identity was taken away from her the very day that she came into this world. She was given no voice. She had come to believe that whatever the parents do, they do it for the good of their children. As such, she had full faith in them and wasn't unduly worried as to what the future had in store for her.

The only thing she was fond of in the entire house was her birdcage wherein she kept some pet birds. She loved them very much. Her love for them wasn't any less than her father's love for her. She used to take good care of them, feed them on time and chatted endlessly with them. If she noticed any bird sad, she'd become upset too and would wait anxiously for it to become better, just as her father used to feel worried when she fell sick. But there was one thing in which they differed from one another. Gudiya used to feel thrilled when she saw the lovely, multi-hued feathers of her birds, whereas Abba used to get worried when he saw the beauty of his daughter. Gudiya's complexion was so fair that it could illuminate everything around her. And this was precisely the reason of his worry. He didn't want people to see her. He didn't want it to become the talk of the town and that is why at such a tender age he handed over a *burka* to her. Initially she wasn't allowed to step out alone. Even if she had to attend any social function like marriage etc., her mother would accompany her and that too under *burka*.

There wasn't much difference between her plight and that of her pet birds, both were happy in their own beautiful cages. Just as her birds wouldn't dream of flying away even if the cage door were to be left open, Gudiya too had got so accustomed to her *burka* that she fell in love with it and could not fathom a life without it.

She got deceived into believing that the birds would never dream of leaving her because they were in love with her. The truth was that they had forgotten to fly in the open boundless skies. Like them, she too had become oblivious of the fact that there existed a real life that was beautiful and carefree. *Burka* and the other associated curbs that had been imposed upon her had become an integral part of her life. She no longer knew what life would be like outside the *purdah*. Even when she went shopping with her mother, her eyes would always be looking for *burkas* of different styles and colors instead of the latest designs of salwar-kurtas that had come into the market. And her Abba also never showed any reservations about her splurging money on them.

Obviously, how could he have put any restriction on restriction itself!

Ghatgate market was the local market that catered to the needs of the women living in that area. There were fewer shops selling salwar-kurtas than the ones selling *burkas*. There were all kinds of them, the net ones, the embroidered ones, the designer ones. The shopkeepers were crafty enough to pass off their local stuff as imported ones from across the border i.e., Pakistan. Women would fall for such ploy and buy them without much ado. Probably they didn't want to be left behind where the latest fashion was concerned.

God alone knew on which part of the hemisphere of our spherical earth this area was situated because the rays of the worldly wisdom always fell obliquely. Here the children weren't much interested in education. Leave aside the girls, even the boys shied away from attending schools and other such institutions.

This was the entire world for Gudiya. She had never ventured out of Ghatgate area where they lived. So how could she ever imagine that there was a whole world waiting outside to be explored. There were numerous countries some hot and sweltering, and others biting cold and then there were seven seas too. But little did she know about them because the places where you study about them, weren't meant for girls like her. Dubai and Arab were the only two foreign countries that she had heard of and that was because many of her relatives had gone there to earn their livelihood. She had never been introduced to the outer world by her parents, so the very thought of crossing the threshold never occurred.

As the date of her marriage drew nearer, Gudiya got engrossed in her own marriage preparations. The meaning of marriage for her wasn't new life or new responsibilities, it meant having plenty of new clothes and new jewelry. She was excited at the very prospect of being allowed to exercise her own choice and not wear what her Ammi wanted her to. She'd be able to wear her brand new brightly colored embroidered salwar-suits and also the bright red lipstick that would complement her strikingly fair complexion.

Gudiya was on cloud nine. One day, her cousin Shaheen came home and congratulated her on her engagement. She very proudly showed her all her clothes, jewelry etc., that were part of her wedding trousseau.

'You silly girl, marriage doesn't mean new clothes and jewelry alone.'

'Then what does it mean? Does it mean that your mother-in-law would beat the hell out of you?' Gudiya said and burst into laughter.

'No, it means having a husband too,' teased her cousin.

Gudiya felt extremely shy. She did not know where to look. A sudden tremor passed through her body and she found herself floating in its ripple along with all her clothes and jewelry.

Night and day, she thought about Waseem only. He had completely taken over her imagination. She would dream of herself dressed in radiant red, held captive in Waseem's loving embrace.

When Ammi showed the engagement set to her, her face turned deep crimson and she lowered her eyes bashfully. A stray lock of hair kissed her cheeks and she hid her face in her palms.

Amma shared her daughter's happiness with her husband saying, 'Listen, our daughter has really liked the clothes that we have bought for her engagement.'

Abba heard that and smiled knowingly. He then cast a side glance at his elder son who was sitting nearby. It frustrated Kareem but he felt completely helpless. He felt that they were rushing headlong into this alliance by marrying off his sister and sending her away to her marital home. They were merely carrying out their obligations as parents and exchanging the old trappings for the new ones.

Gudiya wasn't a burden to be passed off so summarily.

But she, on the other hand, was happily engrossed in her own dream-world. Little was she aware that that life won't do her any good. Nor did she know that all her new clothes and jewelry would enchain her forever. How should he make her understand that these beautiful dreams of hers might spell doom when they collide with harsh reality?

Kareem found it difficult to sit with his Abba in the same room. As he came out into the verandah, his eyes were moist with unshed tears. A gentle touch on his shoulders startled him. He quickly wiped his wet face with the back of his hand before turning back. There stood his little sister in front of him. She looked at him imploringly and said,

'Bhai, please don't worry so much about me. Whatever Abba is doing, he's doing it for our good. Why would he ever think ill for his own daughter? Have faith in God, everything will be fine. Please stop worrying about me unnecessarily. I'll be fine. I don't want any money, so it doesn't really matter whether Waseem has a job or not. And besides that, *Taya* Abba is there. He wouldn't deprive me of food or comfort. And moreover, you would always be there whenever I need any help.'

His sister's naivety and unworldliness made Kareem even more emotional. His eyes brimmed over as he hugged her tightly. How should he make her understand that with Waseem's vagrant nature and his joblessness she might manage to run a household but would never be able to nurture a lasting relationship with him.

The days of fasting had begun. It wasn't easy to observe fast during winters, but wasn't very difficult either. The responsibility for cooking the *sehri* for her four brothers and parents rested on Gudiya's shoulders. She'd wake up at three in the morning and after feeding her pet birds would enter the kitchen to prepare food for everyone as per their wishes and pallets. By 4:15 a.m. everyone would be through with it and after offering the *namaz* they'd all go back to sleep once again.

But sleep used to elude Gudiya. She'd lie awake for hours on end with her thoughts running riot. Since these were the days of fasting and prayers, she didn't want any carnal desires to defile her mind so she used to immerse herself into the holy Koran and keep the devil at bay.

Why should marriages be solemnized during the month of *Eid*!

Despite their best efforts the young prospective couples found it hard to keep their passions and desires under check. Why should it be considered sin to dream about your beau during *roza*? And if she were to seek an answer to her query, what would people think of her? The very thought made her smile. As she tried to rein her wayward thoughts, the days of *roza* slid past one by one.

After the asr *azan*, the call for evening prayers, she would again get busy in the kitchen work and would be left with hardly any time to indulge in her daydreams. Ammi and she would grind fresh spices mixed with onion, garlic and ginger for frying hot pakoras. Once the family members had opened their *roza* and eaten their meals, the mother-daughter duo would find some respite after the maghrib *azan*.

Gudiya would then open the doors of her heart and allow her thoughts to wander freely. Normally it isn't easy for people to control the emotions but for Gudiya it wasn't difficult. She had mastered this art ever since she was a little girl. Like for example, when her thoughts wandered in the direction of school, she'd forcibly bring them under control by looking at the fight between her elder brother and her father. When her thoughts wanted her to play with other neighborhood children in the lane outside, she'd suppress them by pealing garlic in the kitchen. And when she wanted to share the girlie secrets with her friends, she'd humor herself by talking to the closed doors and windows of her room.

It was only after finishing off the daily chores, when she lay down for some rest that she allowed her thoughts to wander towards Waseem. In her childhood days she used to call him "Waseem bhai", how would she address him now that she'd soon become his bride! The very thought made her blush. She'd dream of him showering his passionate love on her saying, 'You are so beautiful that I'd lay the entire world at your feet. Your wish is my command. I'll do everything for you.'

And at this she'd tell him lovingly, 'I only want you to take up a job like a good husband and refrain yourself from simply whiling away your precious time.'

She had a strong feeling that Waseem would comply immediately and very lovingly fulfill all her wishes. He'd stop being a wastrel and start leading a good life. Once she was able to put things right, she'd be able to breathe a sigh of relief for she didn't want her brothers to feel guilty that their father had done something wrong in marrying her to Waseem.

'Gudiya, Gudiya…' she was jolted out of her reverie by Ammi call.

Wearing her dupatta, she rushed towards the kitchen to serve food to Abba and her brothers. She knew that they would have come back home after offering the *namaz*. Ammi served them curry as Gudiya put hot chapatis in their plates. Today she had made some halwa for *iftar*, which would serve as sweet dish.

After that they all sat together to eat their meal. Gudiya finished in a jiffy so that she could help in serving food. As she was about to get up, Abba stopped her midway saying,

'Eh, what's that? Have you finished already? This wouldn't do. Look at yourself. You have become so weak. You should look after yourself properly. Here take this chapati and eat it with me.'

After all these years, this was the first time that she got as much attention from her father. It made her feel rather special. She had absolutely no idea what place she held in Abba's life, if at all. But today, it seemed different.

She bent her head to look at herself. She had always been like that only. Then why was Abba saying that she looked thin? Why was he so concerned? Tears welled-up in her eyes but she quickly pushed them back and went and sat near Abba without murmuring a word. She had never experienced that kind of feeling in her entire life.

Gudiya's appetite for food was satiated, but this hunger was of a different kind. She had always craved for her father's love.

Abba put the *chapati* in her plate and said cajolingly, 'Come on, eat.'

She felt completely dazed by his affection and ate that chapatti even though she wasn't hungry. Every morsel that she ate was soaked in his love for her of which she had been bereft of. She wanted to hug him, rest her head on his shoulders and cry her heart out but she could not. Little did she know whether it would go down well with him or not.

The day was nothing short of a miracle for her. She felt that she had been abundantly rewarded for having observed her *roza* so diligently and expressed her gratitude to Allah for showering his grace on her. And why wouldn't she do that? She had only heard about Abba's love, but had never felt it, till today.

'Amma, Abba really cares for me, isn't it?' she asked her mother, as she lay beside her.

'Yes dear. He loves you since the very day that you came into this world. But he doesn't know how to express it,' replied her mother gently. 'It happens with girls in every household. Fathers aren't able to express their love for their daughters. A man's nature is made that way only.'

Gudiya's eyes sparkled as she listened keenly to every word spoken by her mother.

'Now look at me. It's been twenty-six years since I got married to your father and I'm still waiting for him to say that he loves me. Men are like that.'

'What? He hasn't said it even once?' Gudiya probed.

'Yes, I'm telling you the truth. I kept waiting for years for him to tell me how much I mattered to him or that he wouldn't be able to live without me. I kept waiting for him to tell me how beautiful I was or that I was the best wife in the entire world.' Amma let out a deep sigh and continued, 'But then I understood that men do not say these things. These are very womanish things, things which only women dream about.'

She suddenly turned towards Gudiya and said, 'You also don't nurture any such expectations from your husband. Such dreams hurt awfully when they don't come true. So, don't build castles in the air and allow yourself to be deluded by them,' saying this Amma moved towards her side of the bed leaving her to ponder over her words.

But Gudiya's eyes twinkled with a smile as she tweeted, 'No…I'll dream and make sure that all my dreams come true.' She was in that special zone wherein she felt on top of the world. She didn't want anything to dampen her enthusiasm.

She gazed at herself in the mirror and turned deep red even though she was all alone. It was her very first experience of this kind when she wasn't able to face her own self. Although she was just a fifteen-year-old girl but she felt very womanly from within, conscious of all the transformations that were going on inside her.

The festival of *Eid* was round the corner and so was Gudiya's marriage. The mother-daughter duo would quickly finish off their household chores, pick up their bags and go shopping even though they were observing their *roza*. They'd be seen sometimes at the bangle-shop and sometimes at the goldsmith's selecting jewelry.

They would walk the entire distance on foot from Ghatgate to Ramganj, which wouldn't be less than two to three kilometers at least, because Amma was of the belief that being on foot gives them a better chance at bargaining.

'Amma, Shaheen told me that there is plenty of latest and trendy stuff in *thokbazar*. Let's go and check there too.'

And both of them decided to go to the wholesale market. They went there only once or twice in a year because the things that they required on a day-to-day basis were easily available in the Ramganj-Ghatgate market itself.

By the time they reached the Ramganj crossing, Gudiya started feeling a little tired. 'Amma, let's take a rickshaw. It would be better for you also as we are both observing *roza*.'

'Yes, I was about to suggest that myself. Hail a rickshaw.'

Gudiya, who was covered from head to toe in *burka*, stopped a rickshaw.

'Bhai, we have to go to *thokbazar*. How much?' asked Amma.

'Twenty rupees', said the rickshaw driver.

'Arre, we aren't outsiders! We are locals only. The going rate between Ghatgate and thok is ten rupees only. And you are asking for twenty rupees from this crossing? That's too much.' Amma tried to bargain shrewdly.

'Arre Ma ji, why do you argue during *roza*? Everything has become so expensive these days and you are haggling for a few rupees with a poor man like me,' the rickshaw-puller was equally adept at negotiating.

'It's only twenty rupees Amma, give it to him please', Gudiya pleaded softly in Amma's ears.

'No, no…but I'll not give you more than fifteen rupees,' Amma found a middle path.

The fare was settled and the rickshaw-puller drove them towards the market.

They went from shop to shop, buying things of their interest. It was winter season, but both of them had begun to sweat profusely. Amma was convinced that Gudiya wouldn't leave her till she got her to spend every single paisa in her purse.

'Amma, look at these bangles! The color is so beautiful. I feel like buying a salwar-kameez too of the same color. Amma gave her a side glance and smiled.

'Okay, take it if you like it. Your Abba had categorically asked me not to refuse you anything. And here you are trying to take advantage of me.' Amma chided her indulgently and moved towards the ready-made garments shop to buy a suit that would match with her bangles.

By the time they finished with their shopping, it was nearly 4:30 in the afternoon and both of them were exhausted. Amma quickly hailed a rickshaw for Ghatgate for twenty rupees. This time she did not resort to any haggling although she was quite pro at it.

'Bhai, see! how does this look on me?

Of all her four brothers, she was closest to her third brother Hashim.

She showed him the things that she had bought from the market. He too was equally interested in her purchase and appreciated it all whole-heartedly.

'Wow Gudiya! this shade of green is lovely. And its sparkling sequins will look fabulous on you. My little sister would look like a real doll in this one', said Hashim Miya indulgently.

Gudiya held the suit close to her chest and went and stood in front of the mirror to corroborate her brother's words. Seeing her completely engrossed in the vibrant hues of the clothes that she had bought, Hashim Miya felt deeply moved. She seemed to be under no stress about her prospective life ahead with Wasim.

Hashim Miya wasn't very old himself when Gudiya's marriage was fixed up by his father. He would have been all of twenty years in age. By the time he reached college, he had attained enough maturity about life so as to understand the difference between a well-educated person and a vagabond. That was precisely the reason why he did not much want Wasim to marry his sister. But when he saw Gudiya's joy-de-vivre, all his reservations vanished into thin air and he relented.

He often used to visit the houses of his friends from the same community and was very well aware about the plight of women in his own house and their houses.

As an elder brother he felt that Wasim wouldn't be a good match for her, but somewhere in his heart he also had trust in Abba's decision too.

'After all he is our father. He is our Guardian, our benefactor. He has every right over all his children. After the Almighty, it is Abba who is ranked second for it is he who has brought us into this world. Just as God does not deprive us of his benedictions ever, so how could a father divest us of his blessings?'

Hashim Miya deliberated over and over again about Abba's decision to marry off Gudiya to such a wastrel but however hard he tried; he couldn't see any silver lining.

'Ya Allah, have mercy on our souls. May Abba ever remain a *rehnuma* in Gudiya's eyes too! Help us keep our faith alive. We seek your blessings,' saying this he raised his hands in prayers, completely oblivious of Gudiya's presence behind him.

Leaving the clothes that she was holding in her hands, she came to her brother and held his upraised arms, 'What's the matter, Bhaijan? What are you worried about?'

Hashim Miya was taken aback. Quickly regaining his composure, he muttered, 'No, nothing…nothing at all,' and hurriedly left her.

Before he could leave the room, Gudiya caught a brief glimpse of fear that reflected in his eyes, but was too young to understand the reason behind it.

She heard Amma's voice as she entered the room, 'Take these pink bangles and keep them properly, they got left behind in my bag, dear.'

'Oh yes, I had been looking for them, Amma. I thought I had forgotten them at the shop only. I'll just go and keep them with my pink dress.'

'See, how naïve and innocent she is! For her the only meaning of marriage is colorful clothes and jewelry. Does she know anything beyond that?' the elder brother confided in his younger brother who was sitting next to him.

'Yes, but she's happy, isn't she? What else do we want for her? If Wasim is able to keep her happy, it's fine, otherwise we'll bring her back home.'

'We four brothers would always be there for her', the younger brother said.

'But shouldn't we think about her well-being first? If we find a good match for her initially itself, then we wouldn't be discussing about bringing her back home', said the elder brother gravely.

'Bhaijan, don't be so sensitive. Why do you take everything to heart? Can anyone predict the future? How would we know if this alliance is going to be good or not?' the younger brother countered trifle recklessly. He wasn't wrong either. His line of reasoning left the elder one speechless.

Just then sounded the *azan* from the mosque in front of their house and everyone readied themselves for the evening prayers. Amma also got up to wash her hands and face when the phone rang.

'Hello…'

'*As-salaamu alaykum'*. Amma recognized the voice. It was her elder sister in-law on the line.

'*Wa alaykumu s-salaam, bhabhijan*. Is everything all right?'

'Yes, by the grace of Allah, everything is fine. I just called to check if it is convenient for us to come over today after the *taraveeh* and give the *Eidi* to Gudiya?' she inquired.

'Yes…yes, why not. Come whenever you want to, it's your own house.'

'That's all right. I am telling you about it in advance so that you are well-prepared to welcome us appropriately and extend a good hospitality as well. As you'd be well aware that one does require an advance intimation specially if the in-laws of the daughter are coming over. Isn't it?' Her sister in-law said rather pompously from the other side trying to impress upon Amma her own importance as Gudiya's mother in-law.

Amma understood the underlying sarcasm in her tone. Since she was the elder brother's wife, she rarely missed any opportunity to boss over her. And now her arrogance had risen several notches higher simply because she was taking Gudiya as a bride for her son. It gave her an additional power over their family to demand things to be done her way. She made sure that her directives were adhered to.

'Gudiya, where are you?'

'I was just going to offer the *namaz*. Why? What is the matter?'

Amma said, 'You can do that later in the night. Right now, go and get ready and then come to the kitchen to help me out.'

'Why, what happened? Everyone has finished with their meals, isn't it?'

'Your mother in-law is coming over with your *Eidee*.'

Gudiya was thrilled to hear that.

'Oh wow, this would mean that I'd get another suit, but I'll keep it with my wedding trousseau. I've already got a new one stitched for *Eid*. Besides, I'd also get new jewelry-set and new pair of slippers and make-up box too. But I won't open it right now. I'd be needing it later when I'd be required to attend all those parties after marriage…'

'Eh, what are you doing? Do you intend to serve cold drinks in winter season?' shouted Amma as she saw Gudiya stirring sugar in order to make syrup.

Gudiya was jolted out of her daydreams by her mother's voice and grinned sheepishly at her own self for having forgotten that it was winter time and she had to make arrangements for tea.

She was never a favorite of Badi Ammi, ever since she could remember. She could only recall her condescending nature, who never used to respond to her greetings. That is why she usually kept her distance with her. Although between both the families, Gudiya was the only daughter, but she rarely received any attention or love from her. But *Taya* Abba was different. He was affectionate and he genuinely liked talking to her.

She felt bitter about those times but didn't want Badi Ammi's sullenness to sour her beautiful dreams. So, she immediately brushed all her old memories aside and immersed herself in arranging the refreshment bowls in the tray.

Amma was muttering something under her breath as she took out new tea-set from the almirah. Gudiya knew that she was under a lot of flak from her domineering sister in-law. She would get badly chided if she made any slip-ups. And Amma didn't want to give her any reason to do that and expose herself to a volley of insults.

Badi Ammi's visits always made Amma take-out new cushions, crockery and carpet. Although she stayed just two lanes down the road, but Amma always would try to clean up and polish her house before her arrival. And all her efforts would invariably go waste because before leaving Badi Ammi would throw in such a nasty comment that Amma would be left seething. She never could retort back because of Abba. For he always used to say, 'Whatever she does, let her do. She's elder to us and I don't like anyone insulting the elders.'

Seeing Gudiya cut fruits, Amma forgot all about her own grouses and became emotional. She wanted to shower all her love on her. 'How affectionate she is! What would happen when she goes away? Who'd come running at my call? I'd be left all alone.'

But then she remembered her sister in-law, and her face contorted. She felt resentment welling up inside her. 'How fortunate that woman is!

The light of my life is going to illuminate her house!'

Both of them then got busy in tidying up the room adjacent to the living room. They arranged the cushions and dusted the carpet. This was a kind of a guest room, an extra room that was put to multiple uses. It was here that women guests would be seated. Otherwise, it was used by all the brothers and their friends for lounging around.

This was the place where the family members would generally congregate for their usual chit-chat. Since it was right next to the living-room with one door opening to the street outside, it was also used by Abba's friends from Jaipur to stay over-night whenever they were in town. And when that happened, the door that led to the inner verandah was closed from inside as well as outside in order to maintain privacy for the womenfolk. Whatever the guests needed during their stay like food and other things were taken to them through the outer door via the living room.

Although it was quite a detour for the brothers, but they complied happily for the sake of the women of the house who were able to move freely between their room, kitchen and the verandah without having to face the guests every time.

The mother-daughter duo heard a noise outside and both stood up. It was Badi Ammi outside who greeted them from behind the *purdah*.

Saying '*As-salaamu alaykum,*' Badi Ammi entered the room.

'*Wa alaykumu s-salaam, bhabhijan.* Amma replied pleasantly replacing the earlier bitterness with a warm smile.

When Gudiya greeted her, she caressed her head and blessed her whole-heartedly. 'How are you, Nazma?'

'I'm fine, Ammi. How are you?'

'By Allah's grace we all are fine too.'

The young girls of the neighborhood who had come with her began to put down the gifts they had brought with them in a row.

Badi Ammi called out, 'Be careful, put them properly. Put the gift containing suit in the front and on top of it put the dupatta packet.'

'No, no. Don't touch the suit packet, I'll do that myself only. It's an expensive piece. I don't want even one sequin to come out.'

This made Amma smirk a little, but the very next moment she regained her composure and put her smile back in its usual place.

'Look here, *Dulhan*, here are a total of seven *shagun thal*. I wanted to bring eleven in all, but since there aren't many days left for the wedding, I thought I'll fulfill my aspirations about the rest of the gifts later,' Ammi said raising her eyebrows a little.

But when she saw Gudiya get up to serve water, she made her displeasure amply clear, 'Eh Bi, don't make my daughter in-law work so much. Let her relax and enjoy. As far as work is concerned, the entire life is there. She is here in your house only for a few more days. I hope she is not a burden to you?'

The sarcasm in her voice made Amma cringe hard as she muttered to herself, 'Kareem was right. Gudiya would be much better off remaining single and staying in the same house rather than being married into this family. But how do we find a right match for her now? Since she is the boy's mother, we have to play up to her, otherwise why would I ever go knocking on her threshold and get myself insulted every single time?'

Badi Ammi picked up the beautiful sequined dupatta of the new suit that she had got for her *Eidi* and put it on Gudiya's head. She blessed her whole-heartedly and kissed her forehead to ward off all evil spirits, saying, 'Look, how pretty she looks in the suit that I have brought for her. I had specially asked for it to be sent from Banaras. Look at these sequins, they are so beautiful that they'd get soiled on mere touch alone.'

'It's a very expensive suit. Be very careful while wearing it. All the money would go waste if it gets spoilt,' she cautioned Gudiya.

Gudiya nodded her head timidly.

Then pointing towards the make-up box, she further added, 'This is from Dubai. It came only yesterday. That is why I was a little late in bringing over your *Eidi*, otherwise I would've come much sooner.'

'Anyways, I have handed over the gifts to you and Gudiya. Now it's up to both of you.'

'Now tell me when are you coming over with *Eidi*?' Badi Ammi asked bluntly.

'We would be there tomorrow itself. Till now we were waiting for your visit to be over, since as per tradition, it's the groom's family that comes over first...' Amma began a little cautiously.

'Good, since you know about the traditions, I guess, you'd also be well aware of the fact that the bride's side has to bring double the number of gifts that have been brought by the groom's side,' Badi Ammi completed the conversation.

Gudiya dozed off after offering her early morning *namaz*. When Amma saw her sleeping, she too went and lay down next to her. She hadn't yet recouped from the previous day's tiredness. And today again, she knew, it would be another equally exhausting day as she had to take *Eidi* for Wasim. The very thought of going to her elder sister in-law's house was enough to give her jitters.

Although she had taken all due precautions to ensure that things were as per her wishes and Gudiya's father also had been equally lavish in buying expensive gifts for the groom's family, but still she had that nagging certainty that her elder sister in-law would find some fault or the other. Mulling over these things, she didn't realize when she also dozed off.

It was nearly nine o'clock when she woke up with a start. What would her husband say if he came to know that she had over-slept! Gudiya wasn't there next to her.

As she came out of the room, she saw her chatting happily with her pet birds as she fed them. Seeing her mother, Gudiya said, 'Amma, look after my birds when I'm gone. Or let me take them with me too. I don't know what will I do without them.'

Amma said, 'No darling, let them be here only. We'll take good care of them. Your birds are going to enliven our house after you are gone. We'd feel less lonely.'

'And what would happen if they too fly away one day...'Gudiya asked laughingly.

'How would they fly away? They have already got used to staying in this cage.'

'Yes, I know they won't go anywhere. I have bought such a beautiful cage for them and I also look after them very nicely,' Gudiya said artlessly.

'Yes, darling, there are many birds who don't understand the real meaning of freedom, they get so habituated to captivity.'

'And the caretaker is deluded into thinking that they don't fly away because they love the cage that he has provided to them…' Amma repeated this to herself many times over not knowing why she did that nor what she wanted to prove by it. She then crossed over to the verandah and immersed herself in the task of putting the *Eidi* gifts in a large suitcase that she had emptied.

The previous day she had given her son a list of different kinds of fruits and sweets that had to be bought from the market. She wanted some more things to be added to that, so she called him out.

'Yes, Amma?' said Hashim as he came out in the verandah.

'Bring ten to eleven different types of sweets if possible'.

'But Amma, it would be very difficult to find so many varieties here. This is not Bikaner that you can buy all at one place,' replied her son.

'I don't know how you'd get them, but get them. And yes, bring one packet of dates as well. We'd be able to fill one gift-plate with that.'

'One plate full of dates only?' he asked her incredulously.

'So what? We'll have to be taking at least eleven of them instead of seven that they had brought, otherwise you'd feel slighted in Gudiya's *sasural*. We have to keep our reputation intact.'

Hashim Miya lost his cool when he heard that.

'Then, is it necessary that we take eleven against their seven? It's not obligatory to take more than what the boy's side brought simply because we are giving our girl to them. When would we free ourselves of these laidback traditions?'

'I would overlook it dear, but your Badi Ammi wouldn't.'

Amma then got busy with the other preparations leaving her sons to go to the market to purchase the remaining things.

'One whole generation has passed, still things haven't changed much. Whatever customs and traditions were there at the time of my marriage, are still there in my daughter's time too. It's now my turn to face the same insults that my parents faced at the time of my marriage. God knows when we'd be able to break ourselves free of these constricting shackles.' Amma muttered to herself.

'Amma, you can be the change that you are talking about in others,' Hashim Miya said empathetically to his mother as he entered the room with bags in his hands.

Amma felt a little embarrassed. Behind Hashim, she also saw Kareem standing with sweet boxes. She thought that he'd feel vindicated upon hearing her anguish and would immediately go and confront his father for having chosen such a partner for his sister but to her surprise he did not utter a single word.

Hashim Miya understood the look in his mother's eyes and said, 'Amma, you know that bhai doesn't like this match for Gudiya, then why do you involve him in all the marriage preparations?'

'You people don't know anything. Even if you find another match for her, what's the guarantee that he'd be the right one? Can you re-write her fate? All menfolk are same. Women have no choice but to follow their bidding,' It seemed as if Amma was voicing out her own angst.

Gudiya was all alone in the entire house. Both her elder brothers had still not come back from college and Abba had also left for his office after the Jauhar *namaz*. Amma along with her nieces and some of the neighborhood women had left on foot to go to Badi Ammi's house. And both her younger brothers also had gone there in the car carrying the gift items for the groom.

Gudiya lay on the cot basking in the warm winter sun. It soon became quite hot and Gudiya tried to cover her face with a shawl to escape the piercing rays but it wasn't of much help. She felt too lazy to get up or shift her cot towards the shade to avoid the direct light.

In one corner of the verandah, the home-made vermicelli was drying in the sun and near it was kept Gudiya's birdcage. As the warm rays of the sun fell on them, the birds started chirping excitedly in high pitch. Soon it reached such a crescendo that it appeared as if they were fighting with one another. It disrupted Gudiya's reverie, so she got up and shouted loudly, 'quiet' and all the birds fell silent. She burst out laughing and with a frayed durrie covered the cage so as to provide them some respite from the hot afternoon sun. This brought down their chatter significantly, and made the surroundings serene.

The rays of the sun fell on the red-colored floor tiles and added to its luster. And the gentle breeze made the lush-green leaves of jasmine and lily rustle softly. There butterflies too that fluttered and frolicked around joyously.

On the floor lay strewn the withered flowers of yester evening. These were the very flowers that Gudiya had plucked the previous day to put behind her ears. She could still smell their sweet fragrance emanating from her body. Her eyes sparkled as she gazed towards them. Given a choice, she would want to wear floral jewelry around her neck, hair and wrists. But out of diffidence, she never dared to voice her desires before Abba or her brothers. She wasn't sure of their reaction.

Let people say what they want, but whenever she wore flowers, she felt as if she was in the land of fairies, engulfed by the sweet-scented breeze. Her entire being felt fragrant as her thoughts drifted towards her *sasural*. After her marriage, she wouldn't be answerable to anyone, neither her father nor her brothers. No one would mind if she dressed up nicely. She'd weave beautiful flowers in her hair and Wasim would get completely enamored by her fragrance and say, 'Why do you smell so good? It makes me go insane.' She would then laugh gleefully.

Her love for Wasim was akin to tender blooming buds. It was spreading its fragrance everywhere. For hours she kept loitering around in her dreamworld, enveloped in the heady scent of her new clothes, jewelry and perfume. There was no one else in that garden, neither Amma or Abba, nor was there any fear of anyone stalling her flights of fancy.

In this dream of hers there were no restrictions or limitations of any kind. She could move around freely, go wherever she desired. She could caress the flowers and talk to the butterflies. She could also touch the stars and the moon. There were no curbs, no restraints whatsoever. They were after all an integral part of her dreams. How could anyone ever have the power to censor dreams?

Amma was quite out of breath as she reached her elder sister in-law's house. The *burka* that she had to necessarily wear wasn't of much help either since not a single whiff of air could pass through it. She felt suffocated. 'Whether a woman lives or dies, she is obliged to cover herself in *burka* and veil till her dying day.'

Amma muttered to herself as she stepped in the verandah of her elder sister in-law's house who was soon going to become her *samdhin.* She deftly hid all her bitterness and irritation behind a smile and greeted her with a salaam.

Her sister in-law wasn't any less in theatrics herself. She returned her greeting with double the warmth and a tight embrace. Hashim Miya and his brother followed in with all the *shagun thal* and placed them in the center of the room. Fruits, coconut, dates, vermicelli, nine different types of sweets, sugar-jaggery, dry fruits, bottles of sweet syrup, clothes for Wasim and his parents, shoes and socks, shaving kit, perfumes, handkerchiefs and on and on.

After handing over the *Eidi*, Amma returned home completely exhausted and found Gudiya engrossed in preparing the mince-meat balls for the evening *iftar* as she had asked her to. A scrumptious aroma of roasted spices emanated from the kitchen.

'I feel dog-tired. It's my fast also today.' Amma said as she sat down.

'Then why are you sitting here? Come on, get up. Go and lie down for a while,' Gudiya coaxed her gently.

Amma could not help but smile at the affection in her voice. She said, 'No, not right now. How can I leave the entire responsibility of kitchen on you?'

She felt a tad emotional that soon her daughter would go away to another house. But the very next moment, the thought of four daughter in-laws coming over to grace her house instead, gave her some solace.

'Today would possibly be the last day of *roza*, but there's still a lot of preparations left for tomorrow,' Amma said to Gudiya as she watered the plants.

Gudiya turned and gave her a beaming smile. She had been waiting eagerly for the *rozas* to get over and *Eid* to come as that would set her free. Firstly, she wouldn't have to be on fast and secondly, she could happily indulge in her dreams about Wasim without feeling guilty. The conclusion of *roza* also meant that her wedding, which had been fixed on the 15th day after *Eid*, was just round the corner.

In other words, it meant festivities, festivities and more festivities.

It would be the '*Eid*' of a new life for her. For the first time in her life, she felt ecstatic. She wanted to live each moment to the fullest in the real sense of the word. For years she had remained bound to this verandah trying her level best to live up to her Abba's expectations. Now she could live her life as per her own wishes and desires. The very thought gave her goosebumps. The moonlight seemed to beckon her to an altogether new world where only she and Wasim would be there.

She went to the terrace after a gap of many days and became rather emotional when she saw its floor and walls. She felt liberated and free in the open air. There had been endless restrictions imposed on her by her father and brothers on going there. But since Abba had gone out for some work, she sneaked out quietly after the *Asr namaz*, with the thought of returning downstairs before he came back home. Only Amma was there in the house.

There wasn't any particular reason for going there. It was just that she wanted to take a closer look at the open skies. It was dusk and the sky was clear. The setting sun gave a silvery glow to the whole atmosphere and she loved every moment of it. She just wanted to gather the silver in her eyes and when she did, she felt the glow enter her very being, making her eyes sparkle.

It was a completely novel feeling for her. She couldn't recall when was the last time that she had seen such breathtakingly beautiful sight of the setting sun and the evening skies. She looked towards the adjoining terrace. It was vacant too. It belonged to her childhood friend Alema. As children they used to cross over to each other's sides many a times. They would sit together the whole day during winters and play with their toys. Together they'd eat berries. And during the summer months, they'd sit there from evening till late night playing hopscotch. They'd get a piece of charcoal and draw the game and Amma would admonish them somewhat indulgently for dirtying her floor. Sometimes they'd run around on one-leg and get scolded by Abba who used to say, 'the terrace would fall'. That time they used to wonder how could that be possible with their light weight. What he'd have felt then could be a sense of losing control over the lives of his children. But without any delay the girls would shift over to a different game. They'd sneak in one corner and play with small round stones. There were so many small little games up their sleeves that when Abba scolded them for one game, they'd quietly swing to another one within no time.

Whatever game they both played, Gudiya was always ahead of her friend, but when it came to marriage, she got left behind. Alema got married two years back when she had just begun her thirteenth year. By the time she turned fifteen, she had become a mother of one daughter also.

Her thoughts drifted towards Alema, who had become a completely transformed person post her marriage, always brooding. She no longer laughed or smiled as she used to. Her glowing pink complexion also had paled. It seemed as if she had lost control over her own mental faculties. Every other day her in-laws would barge in and harass her parents accusing them of having married off their insane daughter to their son.

Gudiya couldn't do anything much to console her friend or share her grief. She was too young to comprehend what was gnawing her heart.

As she thought about Alema, tears filled in her eyes and a couple of drops spilled on her cheeks. She couldn't even understand why her childhood friend had stopped talking to her altogether.

'Gudiya, Gudiya...'

She heard her mother calling her name. When she came downstairs, she chided her lightly saying, 'Eh! What were you doing on the terrace? Come and grind some green chutney, it would taste good with parathas.'

With that she handed over a bowl full of spices and coriander leaves to her. Gudiya pulled herself away from Alema's memories and engrossed herself with the task in hand.

After the *Maghrib namaz*, both the mother and daughter waited for an announcement from the mosque regarding the sighting of moon. For on it would depend whether *Eid* would be observed the next day or not.

Gudiya took her mother's hand in her hands and said, 'Amma, after the announcement we'll go to the terrace and see the moon.'

'Eh, that you can see from our courtyard only. Why do you need to go to the terrace?' replied Amma.

'In all these years have we ever been able to see it from here? And what's so special about tonight that it would come and shine over our very courtyard?'

'Besides Amma, this would be the last time that I'd be able to see it from our terrace before going to the in-laws house.'

Gudiya's words hit a raw nerve in her mother's heart.

She caressed her head gently and said, 'Don't worry, I'll ask for your father's permission, then we both will go to the terrace.'

Soon the food was ready and it was time to end the fast. The entire family gathered together and waited patiently in the dining room for the announcement from the mosque, but to no avail.

Gudiya was a little subdued as she sat there with dates in her hand. She didn't want the *roza* to extend even by a single day for it would mean a delay in her wedding by an additional day. And with Abba being there, she could not even dream of giving it up.

She knew that he'd never forgive her even for entertaining such thoughts. For once Allah might forgive her, but Abba would never. He was a god-fearing man who was very particular about observing *roza* and *namaz* and he expected his family members also to follow suit. Amma, however ill she might be, would never skip or abstain from prayers for she was more petrified of her husband than of God.

She always used to say, 'He is Allah, He is Akbar…there's no one equal to him. He is Raheem, full of compassion, our benefactor, our guardian angel. His bounty and abundance are omnipresent. He bestows his grace on us all. Why would he, who is so merciful, ever punish anyone? He loves all his subjects very dearly.'

Hearing this from Amma, Gudiya also never felt afraid of Allah, in fact she began to love him even more.

Even when she erred at times, she had faith in His compassion, she knew he'd forgive all her short-comings. And that elevated her soul from all griefs. It not only made her feel lighter but also deepened her belief further.

'Oh, the moon could not be sighted today, which means it's certain that the fast would get extended by another day,' Amma tried to pull

Gudiya's leg.

'Yes, so what? It's good, isn't it? With an increase in one *roza*, now there'd be lakhs of *rozas* that would be observed. And with that Allah's benediction would also go up by as many times. I would also be able to partake some of it for myself.' Gudiya tried to hide her despair and went down to wash her hands and feet for the late evening ritual prayers.

It was the last day of *roza* and Gudiya was in a happy frame of mind. She didn't find it as an effort at all, nor did her throat go dry for the want of water. She was absolutely certain that the moon would be sighted tonight and *Eid* would be observed the next day. And a fortnight later would be her… she whispered excitedly to herself and burst into laughter.

She then hurriedly changed the flowers that she was wearing behind her ears. Although her mother tried to thwart it by saying that her *roza* would get blighted with its heady fragrance, but Gudiya smiled at her and said, 'God will surely forgive this much, after all I'm still young, isn't it?'

Gudiya, who was keenly looking forward to her own forthcoming wedding, called herself young, but she no longer felt like she used to feel in her childhood days. Her heart danced with joy.

'Amma, as soon as the evening prayers are over, I'll eat my dinner. I won't wait for others to finish, as I have to put henna on my hands also,' Gudiya told her mother excitedly as she prepared the evening meals.

'Why do you want to apply it tonight? Look, it's color wouldn't go away in fifteen days, then how will you apply your wedding henna?' her mother tried to reason it out with her.

Gudiya was crestfallen. 'Oh yes, I had forgotten about that. But Amma, *Eid* would feel so dull without it.'

'I know dear, but can't help it. May be, you can color your finger-tips only and not the palms.'

This middle approach placated Gudiya. she acceded to her mother's suggestion and she went away to soak the henna.

'Amma, you'll call the *mehndiwali* for my wedding, won't you?' Gudiya pleaded with her mother as she stirred the paste.

Amma smiled at her indulgently without either saying yes or no. But Gudiya was pleased that she hadn't refused it outright, which meant that she'd talk to Abba about it and confirm it the next day.

In a jiffy, Gudiya finished all her chores so that she could go to the terrace to see the moon. God willing, she might meet Alema there and they might have a small heart-to-heart chat like good old times.

Wrapped in a warm shawl, Gudiya sat on the cot that was kept in the red-stoned courtyard as she waited for her mother, who was still in Abba's room. 'She is probably asking for Abba's permission,' Gudiya thought.

It had begun to grow dark. During the winter months, there wasn't much of an evening, it straight away became night, making the days even smaller. As the darkness descended on the evening skies, Gudiya's heart also began to sink. There was still a flickering hope within her but it too was gradually getting over-powered by some unknown fear.

The call for the evening prayers was over too and still she hadn't heard anything from Amma. It only meant one thing; her hopes had been crushed once again. Even her one small wish hadn't been granted by Abba.

She felt dejected and ended her fast rather disinterestedly. She then went and sat on the cot that was kept in the courtyard. Raising her head, she gazed at the skies, but tonight no stars twinkled in her eyes. She kept looking in the star-studded skies, but could see no moon, not even its reflection there.

'Gudiya, come in dear, it's cold outside.' Amma called her.

Wrapping the shawl around her, she got up and went inside the room.

'I've lit the earthen fire-pot. Apply henna and warm your hands in front of the fire so that it dries soon', her mother said and pulled the quilt over herself apathetically.

Gudiya felt terribly hurt. She felt betrayed. Something snapped within her. She had never demanded anything for herself, nor complained about anything to anyone. Tonight, there were many unanswered questions brimming in her eyes looking for answers from the very people who had brought her into this world.

The moon on the terrace, the courtyard, the chirping of the birds, her chit-chat with them, the golden sunlight falling on the verandah, the silvery moonlight on the jasmine flowers, the fragrance of the flowers behind her ears, her room, her gripping silences as she faced her Abba, the affection of her brothers, her mother's togetherness, the terrace where she still wants to play 'hopscotch' as she used to do in her childhood days, would soon get left behind for good.

Her marriage date had been fixed long back, and although she was quite ecstatic about it, but it was only today that it dawned upon her that everything that was dear to her would soon get left behind forever. Something broke within her and tears welled-up in her eyes but she didn't want her Amma to see them. It was different when she was a child when she used to cry to arm-twist her into giving in to her wishes.

She also got reminded of her Badi Ammi, who rarely showed any affection towards her. Her short-tempered surly nature was quite difficult to please. On the other hand, although Amma was amiable and loved her very much, but she also never gave in to her wishes. So, the question of Badi Ammi showering her love on her after marriage seemed rather remote.

'What would happen if Wasim too turns out like Abba, then he also wouldn't listen to me, just as Abba doesn't listen to Amma.'

An unknown dread gripped Gudiya's heart.

She felt helpless and burst into tears. Removing the quilt, she sneaked out of the room and sat on the cot that was kept in the courtyard and quietly gave vent to her tears. The moon was still not visible, but the hazy light from the stars gave the place a silver hue.

God alone knows what message the *Eid* moon wanted to convey to her this year! She had sacrificed so many of her precious tear-drops at its altar as an apology for not being able to decipher its real import.

She was grateful to the moon for not being there in the sky tonight, else people would've seen her teary eyes. But she was sadly mistaken. What if the moon wasn't there? She had forgotten about the countless stars that were sparkling in the skies and in its glow stood a dark silhouette watching her from behind the doors. It observed her silently and understood her plight. But it could not offer its shoulder to her to weep on for that would weaken her spirits for all times to come and render her incapable of living a life wherein she might never be able to see the moon. It would be better for her to gradually brace herself for such an eventuality. In her heart of hearts, she also wished for Wasim, her son in-law to become Gudiya's moon and illuminate her life forever. His love and care might make her forget her desire to go to the terrace to gaze at the earthly moon. Empathizing with her daughter's plight, Amma raised both her hands towards the heavens to seek Allah's blessings.

After the misgivings of the previous night, the morning appeared nice and bright. There were *Eid* festivities that could be seen everywhere in the neighborhood as well as within the house. Sweet fragrance was emanating from every nook and corner. In fact, one could smell the aroma of *mithi sivainya* coming from every household.

On the streets outside was a flurry of activity with people scurrying about to buy their household requirements. It seemed as if a weekly market has been set up to lure people in huge numbers with their fabled Alif-Laila stories. But in reality, most of the people were simply rushing towards the *Eidgaah* so as to reserve their place and offer *namaz* as soon as possible, otherwise even in a big city like Jaipur, they soon run out of space.

The first thing that Gudiya did on *Eid* was to go to her Abba and greet him with a salaam. He patted her head and blessed her from the core of his heart. Gudiya's eyes sparkled with unspoken happiness. She was on cloud nine when he gave her a hundred rupee note as *Eidi*. With the note clenched tightly in her fist and her heart overflowing with Abba's love, she forgot all her grouse and tears of yester night.

She found herself in bright and cheerful mood. Her heart pounded doubly fast as her ears attuned themselves to every phone call that was ringing.

She said to herself, 'Wasim also should call up to wish *Eid*. Amma had gifted him a mobile phone as his *Eidi*, shouldn't he use it to give me a call?'

'It has been so many days since our marriage got fixed up, but he hasn't even called me once or sent any message.'

'Yes, he'd also be feeling equally shy. What if he sends a message through someone and it reaches the ears of the elders? What would they say? It would be so embarrassing.'

Like so many other past occasions, this time again, Gudiya was extremely understanding of the other person's point of view and advocated on their behalf with equal ease. She answered all her questions herself.

'But still he should have given a call. He knows the landline number of my house too.'

'Oh no, what would he say if Abba picked up the phone?'

'Why? As if he didn't know that Abba doesn't stay at home the entire day!'

'He knows fully well that it's only Amma and I who are there in the afternoons'

'If he calls, I only would pick up. And if I get to know the timing of his call, I'll try to send Amma elsewhere. Then we'd be able talk for hours at length.'

She grimaced. What a coward Wasim is! He's afraid of everyone.

'But I guess it's better this way. I think he has high regard for the elders. And moreover, he doesn't need to say that he loves me, isn't it? I obviously understand his feelings.'

Thus, she kept vacillating between reproach and defense. Although Wasim's lack of communication irked her but she ended up exonerating him of all blame.

She justified Wasim's apathy in exactly the same manner as she used to justify Abba's dictums earlier. She believed that they both had a right on her life and willingly surrendered herself to their patronage.

There was complete silence everywhere--within the house and outside in the lanes and by-lanes as well. The menfolk had left for the *Eidgaah* to offer *namaz.* There was no traffic on the roads and no noise of children playing in the streets outside. The lanes were so deserted that even the pigeons could hear their own cooing loud and clear. The children also had accompanied the menfolk, so that they could spend their *Eidi* in buying things of their own choice from the fair that was being held there.

The womenfolk, on the other hand, were all busy getting ready. This was the best time for them to visit each other's houses and show-off their clothes, jewelry and their expertise in the art of make-up. Since the men-folk were away, they were relatively free of other household chores and even the *purdah*.

They knew that once the *Eid namaz* gets over, it would be the menfolk who'd be visiting each other's houses in order to wish them. In such a scenario, it would get difficult for women to step out.

This year's *Eid* was extra special for Gudiya. She had worn the salwar-suit that had come from her in-law's house for the first time. The color suited her very much and she looked resplendent. She gazed at herself in the mirror and fell in love with her own reflection. Feeling ecstatic, she went towards the cage of her pet birds who were chirping joyously. But as soon as she reached them, they stopped cooing, expecting their bosom friend to speak to them.

Gudiya raised the folds of her salwar a little bit and jingled her anklets beamingly as if to say, 'See my friends, the tinkle of my anklets is much sweeter than your songs. From now on, the house is going to resonate with these sounds.'

That day Gudiya received innumerable compliments about her beauty and fair complexion from the neighborhood women who visited them. They appreciated whole-heartedly the lovely sequined salwar suit that she wore. Some young girls kept touching the delicately embroidered zari work on some pretext or the other. There were some other shy ones too who eyed it from afar, envying her for having well-off in-laws that she could wear such heavy expensive suits every day.

Gudiya didn't know why but she felt very close to Wasim in that suit. She felt that the fragrance that was emanating from it would be quite similar to the one that she'd feel when they both would be together.

From the next day onwards the hustle-bustle of the wedding festivities began. Everyone tried to contribute towards the preparations. Rolls and rolls of cloth were bought into the house to be given to her in-law's family as wedding gifts from the bride's side. Badi Ammi had handed over a long list of names who had to be welcomed with the gifts. It was a list of 80 sets, 80 for menfolk and the same number for womenfolk. The responsibility to gift-wrap them had fallen on the younger bhaijan. He muttered darkly as he began packing them into new polythene covers adding a fifty rupee note as *shagun* in each packet. The suits and clothes that had come for Gudiya's in-laws were exorbitantly expensive, besides there were gold earrings for her mother in-law and a gold ring for her father -in-law.

Amma picked up the packets that were to be handed over to her in-laws.

'We will have to be putting at least 500/- rupees each in these packets.'

Bhaijan was zapped. He asked, 'Amma, why should we squander so much of cash?'

'Yes, we have to. What's the big issue?'

'Just thank your stars that Gudiya is going into our extended family only. If we had fixed her marriage anywhere outside the family, we'd have been spending much more than this, do you understand?' said Amma.

In the living room, Hashim Miya discussed the menu and the ingredients that would be required for making korma- gulatti with the chef who had been engaged specially to prepare the wedding feast.

'We'd require at least a hundred and fifty kilograms of meat for that. It is my responsibility to cook a delicious mouth-watering dish out of it,' said the chef.

'And how much quantity of gulatti would be made from that?' Abba asked.

'We'll have to buy at least sixty kgs of that. There'll be approximately 500 people for dinner, isn't it?' replied the chef.

'Alright, just make a detailed list and give it to me. I'll get the things delivered. Just see that we don't miss out anything.'

Till now Abba hadn't allocated any work to his eldest son, Kareem. His only work was to take him on his motorcycle to wherever he wanted to go. Both of them would set off together in the morning to give the invitation cards to their friends and relatives and return back in the evening.

Kareem quietly did whatever he was told to do. He neither talked to anyone nor did he complain about anything. He just followed his father's instructions. Since he was the eldest son, that is why Abba took him wherever he went. That way he'd get acquainted with everyone and besides, he'd get his due regards as well since he was the eldest son.

Amma too was immersed neck-deep in the household chores. She worked day and night tirelessly. After finishing off her routine work, she'd sometime sit down to clean the wheat and sometimes the rice sack in the afternoon.

She had engaged the services of a temporary maid so that she also could get some respite. Although Abba was quite against keeping one, but he also didn't want Gudiya to be burdened with any extra work, so he agreed for it for a month albeit unwillingly. Besides her, Amma's sister also used to drop in the afternoons to help out in cleaning the grains and storing them separately in big tin jars.

A list had also been made of the items that were to be given to Gudiya as part of her wedding trousseau viz., T.V., Refrigerator, A.C., sofa-set, double-bed, kitchen utensils...some of which had already arrived by truck. Gudiya was unable to contain her excitement upon seeing that they were meant exclusively for her. Of all the things that were there, it was the dressing table mirror that she liked the best.

'I 'd keep all my make-up accessories in the three drawers and in the narrow almirah on the side, I'd keep my perfumes, scents, kajal, hairbands and shampoos. Although the bangle stand is a little too small, but I'd put some bangles on it and it would look fine.'

She had already begun setting and arranging her dressing table in her dreams. That was the most interesting item from her trousseau. Another thing that she was ecstatic about was the fact that she'd have her very own T.V. set in her room.

'Wasim and I would lie on the bed and watch our favorite serials and programs. There'd be no restrictions from Amma also. The remote control would be in our hands and we'd be able to watch all the latest songs and movies till late in the night.'

'Here Amma never allowed me to watch any of the latest films. She always said that it wasn't appropriate for me.' Her face contorted as she thought about all the restraints that were imposed on her.

The life ahead seemed all rosy, so every word of caution annoyed her.

Amma and *Khala* had readied her wedding attire. It's deep red color with the intricate zardozi embroidery was amazingly beautiful.

Amma said, 'This Katla market is quite a unique place, look at this, we got this wedding *lehnga* at a throw away price. It only costed us two and a half thousand rupees, outside it won't be less than ten thousand at least.'

Khala said that her sister in-law had gifted a similar wedding *lehnga* to her own daughter in-law. She had bought it from Jodhpur for nine thousand rupees.

Both the sisters were deeply engrossed in discussing how their shopping was better and smarter than that of others. But Gudiya was quite uninterested in their conversation. It all went above her head; lost as she was in her own dreams.

She dreamt of herself sitting in all her bridal regalia with a wedding band playing melodious songs and people dancing cheerfully to its rhythm. Her friends would feel envious watching it for they would've never seen such wonderful festivities in any wedding procession before. It would be a grand affair.

And why wouldn't it be grand! Wasim belongs to the present generation and would leave no stone unturned to make it memorable for his friends who'd all be busy practicing their latest dance moves to perform in his barat.

'Would you keep day-dreaming only or help out with tomorrow's preparations also? I'm quite tired managing everything by myself. If it weren't for my sister, I'd have already collapsed by now. The moment you came to know that you'd be leaving this house soon, you have withdrawn yourself from everything. You are only interested in your own well-being. At least take the responsibility of managing your own things.'

Amma tried to ease off her exhaustion through words but ended up taunting her daughter. She continued further, 'Come, take out your yellow suit and if it requires ironing then do it today itself. Or if you have to work on its hemline, complete it now. You won't find any time tomorrow. The guests would start pouring in from morning only.'

Gudiya did not pay much attention to her long sermon. She continued to play with the jasmine flowers. That infuriated her mother even more and she snatched them from her hands and threw them away.

Gudiya looked at her mother with bright sparkling eyes and said laughingly, 'My dear Amma, don't worry so much. I'll take care of everything,' and took out the suit from the almirah.

The entire house came alive with women everywhere as the pre-wedding rituals began. In the evening it was her *Mayun ceremony* followed by a sumptuous feast. The relatives and guests started pouring in from the early afternoon itself.

Amma gave her strict instructions about the code of conduct that she should observe. For example, she should sit quietly in the room only, if her friends and other women tease her about something she shouldn't reply back, should turn a deaf ear, shouldn't laugh out aloud and shouldn't talk too much etc., etc.

Gudiya thought, 'What difference would that make? On normal days also I keep quiet only. So, I don't think it would be difficult to follow Amma's instructions.'

'Yes, but it is true that this is one occasion when you'd really relish the playful banter of your friends, but here too I would have to be discreet. I better pay heed to Amma's advice. I think, it would be for my own good, otherwise why would she forewarn me?'

As was usual with her, she once again gave the benefit of doubt to the other person.

Amma and her sisters were busy in the kitchen, making preparations for rice-pulao that was one of the dishes to be served for dinner. The house was brimming with guests. The entire family of all her three *khalas*, the entire family of both her *phuphis*, all her *chachas* and *tayas* were the special guests present in the house. And Gudiya was in the room, sitting on her bed making a list of all her things and clothes. Her cousins, who were of the same age as her, came into the room and surrounded her.

'Have you exchanged any letters or messages with Wasim or not? How many times did he call you? What gift did he give you for your *Eidi*,' were some of the questions that she found herself faced with. Instead of replying to any of them she simply blushed and smiled. Moreover, she didn't have any answer. If she said 'no' then they'd think that Wasim didn't love her. And if she said 'yes', how would it get interpreted by others, she didn't know. So, she thought it wiser to keep quiet.

Let them draw their own conclusions from her silence.

'We know, he'd be showering praises on your beauty night and day,' teased Mariam *Bhabhi* and the room reverberated with everyone's laughter.

All the cousins sat surrounding her on the bed, leaving very little space for her. Thankfully it was the winter season, had it been summers, she'd have felt suffocated with so many people in the room. Everyone was gunning for the special status of being the bride's sister or sister in-law, so that when the photographs were clicked, they shouldn't get left behind.

There were some who sat very close to the bride. They too wanted a share of the limelight and show-off their beautiful jewelry and dresses. Despite the fact that it was quite cold, none of them were wearing any cardigans or had taken any shawl to keep themselves warm. They knew how to tide over this cold season. What they were concerned with was that their make-up and their jewelry shouldn't go unappreciated.

The preparations for Gudiya's *Mayun ceremony* commenced after the *Asr namaz*. A huge carpet was spread in the courtyard and in the center was placed a small flat chowki for the bride. The strings of the dholak were readjusted so as to get the right beat and with that the sound of the wedding songs along with their rhythmic clapping began to resound in the entire house.

The peppy drum-beats beckoned women and young girls from the neighborhood, signaling to them that the stage was set for the ritual to begin. And without much delay, they picked up their covering wraps and veils and came over to join in Gudiya's *Mayun ceremony*.

Some of the women were busy singing the wedding songs, whereas others were engrossed in talking to each other. In the midst of all this, Farida *phuphi* called out loudly,

'It's time to bring Nazma out of the room for the ritual. We can't delay it any longer for soon it would be time for Maghrib.'

Gudiya's cousins, who were sitting inside the room with her, had been eagerly waiting for this call to bring the bride out. They all became very excited and wanted to hold her hand as they proceeded towards the ceremony area. Each of them vied with the other to be closer to her.

As she entered the hall, for few seconds everything came to a stand-still. She was asked to sit on the chowki that was placed at the center of the courtyard. Then seven *suhagan* were chosen for the auspicious ritual of applying *ubtan* to the bride-to-be. With that the songs resumed once again. There were some women who were in sync with the tune and lyrics while others were going quite off-beat in their attempts to join in. There were some others too who were merely lip-singing for a want of good voice.

Soon Gudiya's hands and feet were completely besmeared with yellow paste. A little later, as she began to feel the chill, her two *bhabhis* stepped forward to rub it off gently.

Then each of the women got up and blessed her by putting some cash amount in her lap as a token of their good wishes for her forthcoming life. Some gave her 100, some 50 and some 20 rupees according to their own financial stature. Then everyone proceeded for a hearty evening meal of chicken biryani and zarda.

Once the ceremony was over, everyone left for their respective homes. But Gudiya insisted with her three cousin sisters to stay over for the night. Amma's sister also stayed back.

Late at night, all the four sisters put the tape recorder on and swayed to the music to their heart's content and applauded each other's moves enthusiastically. They went about it very surreptitiously because playing or listening to loud music or dancing to the film songs was completely forbidden in that house.

Soon the sisters got tired of dancing, fell on the bed and slipped into deep slumber. But for Gudiya, sleep was miles away. For her nights weren't meant for sleeping, they were meant for dreams and more dreams. So, she lay awake late into the night, wallowing in her dream-world wherein she and Wasim were together. Gradually she too drifted into sleep.

'Just four days left for your wedding,' her cousin tried to tease her.

'Four days? Fourth day is the wedding. So, count three days only,' the other one corrected her.

Three days also seemed quite long to Gudiya. She found it difficult to wade through every moment and the continuous teasing of her sisters did not much improve the matter either.

And to top it all, she wasn't able to detach herself from dreaming constantly about Wasim. She found herself held in his tight embrace and however hard she tried to free herself from his grip, he wouldn't relent. The very thought made her blush.

A day before the wedding, when a bride's heart usually goes topsy-turvy with excitement, Gudiya's was extremely agitated.

On the day of *Eid* itself she had pleaded with her mother to call over the henna-artist as she wanted beautiful intricate designs to be made on her palms and somewhere in the midst of it, she wanted Wasim's name to be drawn artistically. She had dreamt that after her wedding when she'd be alone with Wasim, she'd ask him to search for his name on her palms. And when he would see his name, he'd lovingly put his face on her hennaed hands and kiss them gently. But now this dream would remain a dream only, for there'd be no woman to apply henna designs on her palms and no dreams of hers playing these pranks with Wasim would ever turn into reality.

This one small request too had been turned down so unceremoniously. Amma said rather matter-of-factly, 'Your father in-law has sent strict directives that all the rituals should be as per sharia and your Badi Ammi has categorically instructed that both your palms should be fully covered with henna in exactly the same manner as it was at the time of her and my marriage. It is considered auspicious and would bring in lot of good luck.'

Gudiya was very upset. Ever since the day of *Eid*, she had wanted to put some nice intricate designs on her palms, but to no avail. How awful would her hands look! She felt exasperated with all the women who simply wanted to smear henna on her palms. Her heart wept as her limbs went numb under the weight of her own desires.

The day finally arrived for which she had been waiting so eagerly. Although she was still quite dismayed with her red hennaed hands but she somehow distracted her mind by adorning herself, so that at least the rest of her would look beautiful. After all she'd be finally meeting Wasim in person.

She looked resplendent in all her wedding finery with a small *tika* on her forehead and a beautiful nose-ring and necklaces small and big round her neck. The diamond-studded earrings gave a glow to her face. The dark kohl-lined eyes and bright crimson colored lipstick added to her beauty giving her an angelic appearance. When the small pearls at the edge of her zardozi dupatta began kissing her glowing forehead, did she realize how precious was that day for her. She had finally become the bride, the bride of her Wasim.

The colorful glass bangles tinkled on her wrists. And on her ankles, there were silver anklets weighing at least 300 grams each which jingled sweetly as she moved about. Had it been any other day, she'd have removed them immediately. But today it was her enthusiasm and happiness that weighed above everything else.

There were guests everywhere. The wedding ceremony was to take place at 11 o'clock in the morning.

Gudiya sat on the mattress in one corner of her room all decked up as a pretty bride. Amma had asked her specifically to remain silent till all the marriage ceremonies were over.

She believed that at the time of the wedding, one enters a new phase of life, so whatever blessings one seeks from the Almighty at this time surely gets fulfilled.

Each one of her family members had a different advice for her.

Amma said seek from Allah that Wasim gets a regular employment.

Her *Khala* wanted her to seek blessings for her brothers. She said brothers always look after their sisters' well-being, so the first right is theirs.

Farida *phuphi* also threw her weight around and demanded that she should seek blessings for her father's long life.

They had all advised her to seek blessings for either her husband, or father or brothers.

This was what she had been taught from her childhood days that her well-being was dependent on their well-being. Earlier too, whenever she visited *durgah*, she never sought anything for herself. Probably that was the reason she never received any of her due.

Today she wanted to seek Allah's grace and blessings for her own self.

And with her head bowed under the veil, that was exactly what she did. For the first time in her life, she asked for her own happiness. She prayed,

'Allah, fill my life with happiness. Let all my dreams come true. Make my life even better than what I had dreamt of. May Wasim be the person of my dreams, a loving and caring husband, not like the person that my brothers think him to be.'

Tears rolled down her cheeks as she prayed. She desperately wanted to believe that now at least she'd be able to lead her own life as she wanted to.

As she waited, she tried to attune her ears to the outside sounds. She began to speculate as to what would be happening in the wedding procession. She wanted to hear the different songs that would be played by the band. That way she'd get to know all his favorite tracks on which he'd want his friends to dance.

She surmised that the wedding procession would comprise of elephants, camels and horses as is the norm with affluent people. The children who'd be part of his barat would be pestering their elders to ride on them. And the women who'd be walking behind the mare would be wishing for a place to sit in his *baggi*.

The arrangements for the reception of barat was made in the Islamic school nearby. Second floor was ordained for the women and the third for the menfolk. The wedding ceremony was to take place on the ground floor. There were big cannisters filled with juices and syrups. A special arrangement for rose and orange syrups also had been made.

Gudiya's brothers and cousins waited outside the venue with garlands of flowers in their hands ready to welcome the guests from the groom's side.

Despite all the clamor and clutter outside, Gudiya was anxious to hear all that was going on. Then she heard someone asking the womenfolk to put on their veils as *Kazi sahib* was about to come inside.

She wondered what could be the reason for *Kazi sahib's* presence when the barat had still not arrived.

Her cousin sister in-law came and whispered softly in her ears, 'Your *Tai Ammi* has cited Shariya and saved herself a lot of expense of arranging the wedding band.'

'The entire procession is drab and lackluster with no display of any splendor or revelries. The baratis had been reciting Naát Sharif the entire way. It appeared as if they have come for Milad Sharif instead of their son's marriage.' Her sister in-law sneered.

Gudiya was crestfallen again. Just a while ago she had sought Allah's blessings for a happy life ahead but now, another of her dream had bitten the dust. She felt dejected because she would no longer be able to boast in front of her friends about her own 'never-heard-before' wedding festivities.

She was infuriated with her Badi Ammi and wanted to confront her. How could she pinch pennies in her own son's procession? Why did she shatter her dreams: her dreams of a Prince charming who'd come riding on his horse to marry her? Why did she make her a butt of joke before her own friends?

There were sniggers and scoffs all around as everyone made fun of the wedding procession. It became the talking point. She could hear her maternal aunt rolling with laughter saying, 'I had heard that Jaipur is a much bigger city than Jodhpur and people here are also much more educated, still look at the way they bring their barat, it seems they have come to attend *Urs*.'

The maternal aunt's insolent laughter needled in Amma's ears, but she deliberately avoided a retort because she didn't want any sort of unpleasantness in her daughter's wedding. Instead, she willfully diverted her attention towards the cleric's visit.

When two women drew a white sheet in front of her, did she come to realize that *Kazi sahib* had arrived.

In the presence of two lawyers, *Kazi sahib* asked her willingness to be joined in holy matrimony to Wasim for the *mehar* of Rs. 1100/- to which Gudiya replied in affirmative. He then got her signatures on the Marriage Certificate and left after congratulating her.

After that Gudiya's veil was lifted and she was asked to read a page from the Koran. With that she stepped into a new life as a married woman.

The moment it dawned on her that her old life was getting left behind, she burst out crying. Amma who was sitting next to her also could not hold back her tears. She embraced her daughter and started weeping too. In all these years they were the ones who were always together as constant companions, now the time had come for them to part ways.

Both felt lost. Amma was miserable for she would be left all alone and Gudiya was glum for she'd be deprived of the warmth of her mother's affection.

Both had an identical life-journey in that house and that was dancing to the tune of Abba's whims. Their entire life was all about towing his line, following his dictums. If anything was different, it was her four brothers.

Gudiya had blindly accepted all the customs and traditions of this house right from her childhood days. Now that she was married, she would have to leave this life behind and enter a new phase, wherein again she would have to prove her worth and emerge with flying colors. Both of she and her mother dreaded that moment.

Amma knew quite well that her elder sister in-law was more of a conformist than Gudiya's father. When she had known her nature so well, why did she hand over her innocent daughter to her? She could not help but curse her own self.

The house was packed full of women. As soon as the lunch was announced, they began to move towards the nearby school where the arrangements had been made. As the crowd thinned out a little, Gudiya lay down on her bed to relax. Her thoughts invariably took her towards the new life that awaited her. She had known Wasim since she was a child. He had grown into a tall and well-built person with fair complexion and light blue eyes. Amma always used to say that it is futile to expect fidelity from people with light-colored eyes. She used to say this probably because Abba also had light eyes.

But she loved Wasim's blue eyes and wished that she too had them. She felt that they would have made her look even more beautiful than she already was.

After lunch, began the ritual see-off ceremony wherein all the relatives from her in-law's side were given farewell gifts. Badi Ammi's eyes shone with pleasure when she received her gift of gold earrings. Once all the relatives were handed over their gifts, it was time to felicitate the groom.

When Gudiya heard Wasim's name, her heart did a somersault. The very thought of his proximity made her feel ecstatic. He was presented a gold chain, a gold ring, a sterling silver coconut and a cash of 5100/-

rupees as parting gift from his in-law's family.

The women present there looked at each other, for it was rather unusual to give such a princely salami to a groom. But Wasim and his mother did not appear too pleased with it, on the other hand.

As soon as Amma handed over the silver coconut and 5100/- rupees cash amount, Wasim jested, 'Arre, what was the need of giving all this? It would have been much better if you had given me a motorcycle instead.'

Amma was dumb-struck.

The mother-son guffawed loudly to show that it was all meant in good humor, but the barbed comment pierced the hearts of Amma and Hashim Miya. Kareem too moved away from there without uttering a single word.

When the incident reached Gudiya's ears, she was taken aback. She refused to believe that Wasim could say such a thing and said to her cousin, 'He is quite witty, I'm sure, he would have said it in a joke.'

'Oh, come on, we also can understand what he meant. He wanted a motorbike,' her cousin retorted back.

Gudiya was angry with her for blowing things out of proportion. She was unnecessarily making a mountain out of a molehill.

'Badi Ammi might be very ill-tempered and irate, but they have enough and more money of their own. She would never demand a motorcycle from her own brother in-law.'

Soon it was time for her to depart. One of her cousins took out a *burka* from the case that was a part of her trousseau and began to unpack it.

Gudiya had been wearing *burka* since she was eleven or twelve years old. But today, its very sight annoyed her. She didn't want her beautiful wedding *lehnga* and make-up to get concealed by it. And besides, her jewelry too would get entangled in it. She felt helpless and agitated.

Her mother too became emotional as the time to bid her daughter goodbye drew closer. She knew that soon she'd become a stranger to the house and would visit them only as guest. She was apprehensive too about what the future had in store for her and kept praying to Allah for her happiness.

Her brothers too looked anxious as the time of her departure drew nearer. She was well aware of the reason behind their anxiety and wanted to assure them that everything would be fine, but tears choked her throat and no words came out.

As she sat in the backseat of the car, she glanced around from under her veil and saw her mother in-law sitting next to her and her mother in-law's sister sitting in the front seat next to the driver.

She sat with her head bent, clutching the veil in her hands. All her life she had dreamt of Wasim and herself sitting on the backseat, driving towards a life of happier togetherness. He would tease her and she would tease him back by moving away. Lost in her own thoughts, she didn't realize when the car reached the gates of her new house.

The Koran sharif was brought out and placed on her head by Badi Ammi to welcome her into a new life. Wasim also came and stood behind her. She came to know as soon as her mother in-law began to include him in her blessings. His very presence made her heart race.

She was then taken inside a big hall which was Ammi's sitting room. A heady scent emanated from everywhere and there were people bustling around joyously showering blessings and wishes for a happy married life. She was asked to sit on a cot that was covered with a silken bedspread.

As she sat there with her head bent and a veil covering her face, her glance fell on her hennaed palms. They looked awful. It felt as if she was wearing crimson gloves. She immediately hid them under her dupatta and said to herself, 'I'll make sure that Wasim doesn't see them.' She didn't want him to see anything that was bad to look at in their very first meeting.

With every passing moment she grew more and more anxious. She kept arranging and rearranging her *lehnga* and dupatta. She would sometimes glance at her bangles and sometimes adjust her necklace. Then her eyes fell on her feet. She had worn the toe-rings for the very first time and she loved it.

The women lifted her veil and showered praises on her beauty, but Gudiya wasn't much interested in that. All that she was interested in was to hear praises and compliments from Wasim and only Wasim.

There were so many things that she wanted to share with him, so much to talk about, so much to complain and so much to love…

She said to herself, 'Why should I ruin my first night with him? I'll reserve all my grouses for some other day for if he gets offended, then the entire night would evaporate only in placating him.'

And thought, 'The bed decorated with flowers would be awaiting me. There'd be thousands and thousands of jasmine buds spreading their fragrance all around…'

Gudiya then found herself all alone in a room. As she waited for Wasim, she glanced around-there was nothing that even remotely resembled the flowers. The bed on which she sat and the maroon-colored velvet bedspread that was thrown on it were also part of her trousseau. She missed the presence of jasmine flowers dearly. But tonight, there were no flowers in her hair and there were none on the bed either.

She quickly pushed aside her wayward thoughts and realized that her heart had begun to beat wantonly. Wasim would come into the room any moment. He'd try and lift her veil, but she'd tease him for a while. When he'd get tired of it, he would offer a nice gift to her as 'munh-dikhai', may be a gold ring or bangles, she fantasized.

She was lost in her own dreams when she heard the door open.

'*As-salamu Alaykum*...'

She heard his voice and her heart missed a beat. Before she could lift her eyes and catch her breath back to respond, Wasim was heard saying from the other side once again,

'What's the matter? Is there something wrong with your ears? I greeted you and you did not reply…,'

She was hugely embarrassed. Her voice quivered as she replied, 'Wa alaykumu s-salam'.

The voice that came out was so soft that Wasim could barely make out that she had replied back.

'I can hardly hear your voice, seems you have caught cold,' said Wasim as he came and sat next to her.

Startled, she retracted back a little. But the very next moment two powerful hands clutched her and lifted her veil roughly. As she struggled to free herself, he put his face against hers and began to kiss her. Gudiya got no opportunity whatsoever to get a grip on her feelings. His breath which reeked of betel leaf and cigarette began to merge with her breath and she felt nausea rising within her. She tried hard to extricate herself from his grasp but it was all in vain.

It was dark. She could not see Wasim's face, but knew that he hadn't shaved. He continued to rub his coarse unshaven face against hers, bruising her cheeks. Gudiya felt thoroughly hurt and brutalized by this sudden onslaught. Just when a shriek was about to escape her mouth, down came Wasim's powerful hand and clamped it down and she began to gasp for breath. It was her very first experience of its kind.

She felt completely overwhelmed by it and her entire body began to throb. She closed her eyes and soon she became oblivious of his smelling breath. Her arms involuntarily went around him and gripped him in a tight embrace as he bent over her.

Despite the chill in the weather, she could feel Wasim sweat profusely. When he pulled himself away for a brief while, she felt extremely mortified and tried to regain her senses by turning over to the other side. As she struggled to put on her clothes, she was once again pulled back under the quilt.

She stole a glance towards him. In the dim light of the night bulb, she noticed that he had actually not shaved. The least that he could have done was to have groomed himself for his own wedding.

The entire night she was pounced upon and treated like a plaything by her husband and by the time it was morning, every pore of her body felt sore. She who had fantasized about these tender moments all her life, couldn't believe how very painful they'd turn out in reality. Her head began to throb.

She must have finally dozed off around 4:30 in the morning when she heard someone knocking at their door. It was her cousin sister in-law asking her to get ready and come outside. The entire next day too she was kept busy by the continuous influx of women from the neighborhood who dropped in at random, lifted her veil, saw her face, gave her the *shagun* and went away.

She found the entire experience quite cumbersome. Amidst all these things her sister in-law asked her mischievously, 'And what did Wasim give you in *munh dikhai*?' This startled Gudiya and set her thinking.

Wasim hadn't given her any gift on their first night together. In fact, he hadn't even lifted her veil tenderly or even looked closely at her. He, for whom she had taken so much pains to make herself beautiful, hadn't noticed her at all.

Her sister in-law again nudged her teasingly, 'Come on, tell us. Don't be shy. Bhai would have given you a very nice gift, isn't it?'

Without lifting her head, she just murmured softly, 'No, he hasn't given anything yet.'

'Come on…how can that be possible! We aren't strangers that you want to conceal things from us. If you don't want to tell us about it, then don't,' her sister in-law pouted making her displeasure amply clear.

Gudiya felt it wiser not to say anything, so she kept quiet.

It was soon going to be night again. Her heart began to beat doubly fast. She felt thrilled with the thought that tonight again Wasim would take her in his arms and make her forget everything. Although the very thought of his tobacco-filled breath made her flinch, but she didn't want anything to come between their love.

She laughed at herself, unable to comprehend her own whimsical emotions. She simply wanted to keep wallowing in its heady sensation every second.

Gudiya made up her mind that tonight she would definitely ask Wasim to shave his beard before coming into the room. She would also tell him to refrain himself from chewing betel-leaves and smoking cigarettes. 'Right now, I would only request this much of him, gradually I'll make him give up this bad habit also.'

She was again in her room at night when Wasim entered the room. He sat next to her and asked, 'How was your day without me?' Before she could respond, he again clutched her to his chest and did not allow her any rest the whole night. She was numbed by his continuous onslaught and tried to doze off in between only to find him on top of her again.

She felt drained of all energy and wanted to say 'no' to him, but could not utter a single word through her lips. She did not want to risk his anger, so she just closed her eyes and yielded herself to him. By the time it was morning she had begun to detest it all.

Tonight again, there was no conversation between them. He neither spoke nor listened to her. Another couple of days passed by and things remained status-quo. Gudiya wanted to share her heart with Wasim, but did not find the right opportunity to do so. Gradually a thin layer of dust settled on all her desires, and the chasm between them widened even further.

She finally got some reprieve from her busy schedule once the relatives left for their respective homes and the influx of neighborhood women frequenting their house also dwindled. Finding herself alone in the room, Gudiya breathed a sigh of relief and stretched herself on the bed to relax.

She began to think, it would be so nice to meet Wasim during the day time also. It would probably give her an opportunity to confide in him. At night, he rarely allowed her to speak.

She carried on an imaginary conversation with him like she used to do before her marriage wherein she dreamt about sharing her innermost desires with him, but it did not get translated into reality. Wasim had appropriated her body, but could not touch her soul.

She continued to bask in her own fantasy-land, teasing and tantalizing Wasim through her playful banters. It kept her mind occupied all the time whether she was working in the kitchen or sitting in her room during the afternoons.

Thus, during the day time, although Wasim was not physically present with her, he was still there with her in spirit and at night though she was with him, but she still felt aloof. She found herself much closer to the person of her dreams.

Twenty days later, she got her menstrual periods. As soon as her mother in-law came to know about it, she made her displeasure amply clear.

'In the very first month only, I had missed my date. But today's girls are very smart.'

She began to reprimand Gudiya, 'Tell me, are you on any pills?'

Gudiya was stunned, she continued to look at her.

'No, I've not taken any medicine.'

'Then what's wrong with you? How did you start your monthly cycle? I was eagerly looking forward to hearing the good news this month. But how would that matter to you?' She admonished her again.

Her behavior perplexed Gudiya. She failed to understand what mistake she was supposed to have committed.

And by the time it was afternoon, her brother Hashim Miya was sent for. Badi Ammi came in and asked her to pack her things, telling her to go to her parental house for six-seven days. She was shocked as to why she was being sent home in this manner but was also happy with the fact that she'd be able to spend some time with her mother and get some rest as well.

As she began to pack her clothes in a small bag, she thought about her husband, Wasim- 'How can I leave like this? He's not at home right now. He might not like me to go away without his permission. He might not want to send me.'

She was lost in her thoughts when her mother in-law came into the room, 'Come on, wear your *burka*, your brother is ready to leave.'

'But Badi Ammi, I haven't asked him till now?'

'Don't worry about him. I have already told him. You go.'

Gudiya was both shocked and disappointed that Wasim did not even bother to come and meet her despite knowing that she was leaving for her mother's house. His indifference hurt her but she soon forgot about it in the warmth of her mother's embrace when she reached home.

After meeting Amma, she headed straight towards her pet birds who were sitting languidly in the hot afternoon sun. As soon as they saw her in the courtyard, they began to chirp excitedly.

Amma also was equally excited. She'd be able to have a heart-to-heart talk with her daughter for the first time after marriage.

She probed, 'How's Wasim? Everything is fine, isn't it?'

Gudiya understood what Amma wanted to hear. She said, 'He's fine. He's good. Both Badi Ammi and Wasim are good, I don't have any problem there.

But I don't know why Badi Ammi was in a very foul mood today? She was very angry when she got to know about my periods. I didn't like that at all,' whined Gudiya innocently.

Amma smiled, 'Every son's mother wants to hear the good news in the very first month of his marriage. She was annoyed because her wishes could not be fulfilled. Don't worry, it happens sometimes.'

'Yes, I didn't let it affect me, but obviously I felt hurt by her behavior.'

'Don't worry. Everything would be fine. Now take some rest. You look extremely tired.'

Her mother's remark made her conscious of herself but without giving it a thought, she went off to her room. She slept soundly that day. Neither Wasim's thoughts nor his apathy played the spoil sport. She was back in good old days, savoring every moment of her stay.

'Get up, Gudiya, it's almost time for *Maghrib namaz*.'

When she did not pay much heed, her mother came and removed her quilt.

Gudiya said, 'Please Amma, at least you let me sleep peacefully.'

'Alright, but first observe the evening prayers. You know it's not a good sign to sleep at this time. And moreover, it's time for Abba's return. Meet him first and then you can go back to sleep.'

Rubbing her eyes Gudiya got up and pulled the quilt over her feet once again as Amma disappeared into the kitchen to finish off her work.

It had been four days since she came home. In these four days, Wasim did not come to meet her even once nor did he call her.

'How can he stay without me for so long? As far as I'm concerned, I keep thinking about him all the time. But he hasn't inquired even once about me. The least that he could do is to call me up to fight as to why I left without his permission.'

The next morning, Badi Ammi telephoned. Gudiya's heart missed a beat. She thought she'd ask for her daughter in-law to be sent back and she did.

Amma came and told her that Wasim would be coming to pick her up. Gudiya was elated when she heard that. She felt she had wings and was soaring high in the sky. It would be her very first experience of riding pillion with him on his bike. Wasim did come around 2 o'clock in the afternoon. He sat in the outer room with Abba and also had his lunch there only.

Gudiya wanted him to come inside and inquire about her well-being, but he neither came inside nor did he send for her to come outside.

Abba came in and said, 'Wasim has left because he had to go out with his friends. He has given his consent for her to be sent back with Hashim.'

Gudiya was crestfallen when she heard that.

Wasim did not seem to be fitting into her dreams at all. She sat on Hashim Miya's bike and returned to her in-law's house feeling dejected.

She felt like crying her heart out as she sat on her bed. All her dreams and desires were getting shattered one after the other. Each morning brought in new hope only to be crushed with the approach of the evening.

She was reminded of her friend Alema, who used to say, 'Men as husbands become very callous and cold. The wounds they inflict on body and soul can smother anyone to death.'

Wasim finally came home around midnight that day. For the first time since their marriage, Gudiya did not wait for him to come into the room. She lay on bed and covered herself with a quilt.

'You have had enough rest Maharani; won't you even get up and welcome your husband?' Scoffed Wasim as he threw his jacket and muffler aside.

Gudiya got up quietly and greeted him. Wasim pulled her in his arms roughly without wasting any time in sweet-talks making her forget all her grouses. The desires that had gone cold, got re-ignited in the warmth of his proximity as she also embraced him back.

Thus continued their relationship. Gudiya would invariably push into oblivion all his earlier indifference and melt into his arms to savor moments of togetherness.

After gratifying himself, Wasim slipped into a sound sleep. Gudiya sat next to him watching intently as he began to snore heavily.

Over-grown beard, tobacco and betel-stained teeth that had yellowed down, dark circles under his eyes and sweat reeking of smoke.

Gudiya asked herself, 'Is this the prince charming of my dreams?'

She felt nauseated with her own self for sleeping with such a man every night. Once again, she was unable to share her feelings with him. Her grievances remained buried within her heart; they could not see the light of day.

Wasim rarely used to come home in the afternoons. Whenever he did, he'd just come, speak with Badi Ammi and return back. Gudiya sometimes served him food or tea but that too from under her veil only. After that she'd retire to her room and get bored. She found it difficult to pass her time. There was no television set wherein she could watch some serials or films and entertain herself. Although her parents had gifted her one, but on the third day itself, after their marriage, it got installed in her mother in-law's room and her old set was shifted to the living room.

As she was new to the house-hold, she couldn't resist the move. She thought that once Wasim was in a more amiable mood, she'd ask him to put it in their room but the right opportunity always eluded her.

It had been two months since their marriage, but they had barely spoken to each other. Yes, once in a while, Wasim would ask her if she was fine or if she needed anything or if she was happy living with him. He used to ask her for sure, but before she could utter a single syllable, he would deftly maneuver the conversation into a different direction and end the topic.

One day, as soon as he stepped into the room, Gudiya blurted out, 'Whenever you come to me, please abstain from chewing tobacco and betel-leaf, I don't like it.'

This maddened Wasim and he started shouting at her, 'You don't teach me what's good and what's not.'

'You are my wife, not my mother.'

'I'm your husband and not a slave goddammit, that you order me around. My friends are right when they say that wives should be dealt with an iron hand. If you indulge them too much, they start dancing on your heads.' Saying this he shoved her hard against the bed.

She was stunned beyond words. She could not understand what had infuriated him. In all these days that they had been together, this was the only request that she had made to him and he was behaving as if she had committed some huge blunder.

With the arrival of autumn season, the trees had begun to shed their leaves and the cold winds had gradually lost their severity. The March sun too had become rather warm and the woolen sweaters and quilts were no longer required. It was time to put them back in the trunks until the next winters after a due wash. The lighter mattresses felt more soothing on cots.

The days too had become longer which added to Gudiya's woes. Besides, her mother in-law always used to be in foul mood. The real bone of contention was her menstruation cycles every month that led her to raise hell every time she came to know about them.

'Tell me the truth, girl. What medicines are you taking? Is it from a doctor or a quack? What use are you to us if you can't give us an heir? I have not brought you into this house as a mere decoration item.'

'You barren woman...'

The sting of her mother in-law's words impaled young Gudiya's heart and womb through and through, making her writhe in pain. Without uttering a word, she collapsed on a chair and stared vacuously at the traffic that was gliding past.

She was deeply hurt. Those weren't mere words; they were like molten lava which had branded her very soul. She began to moan inwardly at her own plight. And once the tears began to roll down her cheeks, there was no stopping them. She felt as if someone very dear had passed away, deserting her to the mercy of the heartless world.

Gudiya's grief was inconsolable. It dawned on her that her very existence was fake. It was nothing but an illusion, she was as good as dead to the world outside. All these years she had been merely lugging the weight of her own dead body. For years and years, she had been deceived into believing that she was alive. She did not exist at all She was nothing but a walking corpse.

Even the ones who had given her birth, had failed her. They had failed to keep her existence alive. For them she was nothing more than a clay-doll with no likes or dislikes of her own. It was her parents and brothers who took all the decisions for her. They were the ones who dictated how she should conduct herself before others, what she should wear and what she should not. Did they ever look into her heart to see what was it that she really desired?

Abba just happened to say one day that she should stop going to school, and she had to stop. Before she was old enough to understand, *burka* was forced upon her. In the name of fulfilling their responsibility, they had married her off at a tender age and shifted their burden on to someone else. Nobody even regarded her as a human being, regarded her as a live person who could also have feelings.

Today she came to realize that she had been brought into this house with the sole purpose of 'procreation,' to carry forward their lineage. She was brought to cater to the needs of her in-law's family, do all the mundane household chores for her Badi Ammi. Apart from that she had no existence.

Her husband Wasim, also had failed miserably in keeping her 'existence' alive. She was nothing more than a plaything in his eyes, who was only there to provide him his physical gratification and pleasure.

One fine day, Hashim Miya decided to drop in at his younger sister's house. He took with him bags full of fruits and sweets with him as he could not have gone to meet her empty-handed.

When he greeted her mother in-law with a 'salam,' she scowled at him and left him alone in the living room with his sister. Hashim Miya found her behavior rather strange. He glanced towards Gudiya and before he could voice his concern, he clutched his heart in his hands. The ground shook beneath his feet.

Gudiya looked very pale and unwell. He took her hand and made her sit down next to him and asked, 'What happened? Is Badi Ammi upset with you for any reason? Are these people abusing you? You have become so weak? Look at yourself, how pale your face looks. Come, I'll take you to a doctor.'

There came a volley of questions one after the other.

Gudiya lowered her head and said, 'I'm alright, Bhaijan. Let's not talk about Badi Ammi, she simply loses her temper once in a while for no good reason.'

'No, something is definitely wrong. What it is? Don't hide things from me. How is Wasim's behavior towards you? Does he also lose his temper in this manner?' He probed further.

'Don't worry, bhai. It is nothing. These things do happen once in a while in every household.' Gudiya tried to appease him, but could not succeed.

As soon as Hashim Miya reached back home, he went straight to his mother and said, 'Gudiya is not happy there. She looked quite unwell, but she did not share anything with me. Maybe she'd confide in you.'

Amma telephoned her daughter.

On the other side was her *jethani*, Gudiya's mother in-law who picked the call.

'As-salamu Alaykum, *Bhabhijan*,'she greeted her.

'Wa alaykumu s-salam.'

'How is everyone at home?'

'How would they be? Your son must have surely shared with you everything that your daughter fed him.'

Amma was taken aback with this affront, 'No, No. Hashim did not tell me anything.'

'I know you all very well, the kind of people that you are. You have wedded your barren daughter to my son, and now you are insinuating that we don't treat her well.'

Amma was stunned. She felt as if someone had poured hot molten lead into her ears.

But she immediately recouped the situation and said, 'Why do you talk in this way? They haven't been married for long. It's only been six months.'

'So, does it take years to become pregnant? You and I had conceived within our first month itself. And your daughter, on the other hand, keeps getting her menstrual cycle every month.'

'If that is the case, then let's consult a doctor,' proposed Amma swallowing the barbed sting of her words.

'What will a doctor do? And if you are so interested in showing her to the doctor, you take her yourself and consult with him.' And she banged the phone on her.

Amma's hands shook as she put the receiver back. There were tears in her eyes.

After the evening meal was over, she went to her husband to apprise him of the situation.

'What's the matter?' he asked.

'I have to talk about Gudiya.'

Abba became all ears. He asked, 'Why? What happened?'

'Gudiya's mother in-law is furious because she hasn't been able to conceive till now.'

'But what is there to worry or get angry in this? It's only been six months, isn't it?'

'But your sister in-law is all worked up, and has kicked up a big storm in the house. I really don't know how my daughter would be coping up with her nasty temper.'

'I think we should wait for some more time. And besides, doctors are always there. These days there's a cure for everything. You don't have to worry and ask Gudiya also not to take it to heart,' assuring her he turned on the other side.

Wasim, on the other hand, was least concerned about the underlying tensions and problems of his own household. He would come home late at night, indulge in his own sexual gratification and sleep off. Gudiya wanted to talk to him, although she knew that nothing would come out of it. She also knew that instead of comforting her he'd pick up another fight and bully her.

So, whenever she felt lost, she used to indulge in an imaginary conversation with him in order to conciliate herself. The Wasim of her dreams was much more humane. He would smile and listen to her chitchat and kiss her tears away. He would hold her hands in his and promise to fulfil each little wish of hers. He would embrace her and make her the happiest woman on earth.

Her dreamworld was at logger-heads with the harsher realities of life. The only thing that Gudiya wanted was to build an alternate world for herself in some far-off land where she could be forever happy.

But would that wish ever come true? Probably not, for this is a man's world where a woman's dreams are of consequence. Her very entire existence is rendered meaningless!

One full year passed in this manner. Gudiya continued to adorn Wasim's bed, providing him his physical gratification, but she failed to conceive. Her condition deteriorated with each passing day. She became extremely feeble and pallid, but Wasim remained completely oblivious to her plight.

'Wasim, I don't have much expectations left from this barren woman. It is high time you should now start thinking about extending your family,' One day Badi Ammi suggested as she served food to Wasim.

He simply laughed out aloud and said, 'Don't worry Ammi, when the time comes, your wishes would be fulfilled.'

Wasim started coming home very late in the night. It would be nearly two o'clock by the time he'd finally come into the room. God knows by when he would sleep, but one thing was certain. Whatever time he came, he would never forget to awaken Gudiya from her deep sleep. Although she detested that habit of his but couldn't do much about it. She knew it was pointless to resist. For if she did, he'd fight with her and get physically violent. She had no strength left to take any more of his beatings. So, she surrendered meekly to the situation.

She had honed the art of reconciliation very early in life. Frightened as she was of Abba, she had learnt to compromise with various things to meet his approval. And today too, that acquired flair had enabled her to keep her household together very prudently.

In her own heart of hearts, she was grateful to her father for making her the kind of person that she had become, saying, 'If you hadn't imposed all those restrictions on me, I wouldn't have been able to live through this suppression.'

It was difficult to say whether she was actually indebted to him or was dismayed with his upbringing.

It was a full moon night and the moon was clearly visible from her window. It brought a smile on her otherwise pale face, she felt she was meeting her long-lost friend.

'I could never meet you earlier for Abba had imposed innumerable restrictions on me. He was afraid that I might probably get mesmerized by your beauty. But charming as you are and so full of ethereal glow that whoever sees you would get besotted forever.'

The moonlit night reminded her of fairytales that she had heard from her Amma-tales of princess and demons, tales of old women and wild forest. Her eyes filled with unshed tears as she pleaded with moon, 'Why don't you come into my bosom? Then I too would narrate all those wonderful stories to you.'

The maternal feelings that lay dormant within her, came to the fore and tears rolled down her cheeks for hours on end as she sat there clutching her bosom in her arms.

Gudiya was approaching eighteen. It's the age when one leaves the childhood behind and crosses over to the threshold of youth. But for Gudiya it wasn't so. She had moved much beyond that. In the three years of her married life, she had lived an entire lifetime: her childhood, her youth and the life after. She had, in fact, matured much before her time and was now like an abandoned old woman who had been rendered voiceless by her own people. Her status in the house was akin to that old man who had been discarded by all and sundry and was merely counting his last days before he dies. The others too, whenever they raised their hands in prayers, it was only to seek deliverance from him.

She gradually turned into a recluse. Nothing interested her, neither the tinkling of her own colorful bangles nor the sweet sound of her anklets, neither the lovely fragrance of the blossoming jasmine flowers nor the prospect of engaging into a small tête-à-tête with her pet birds.

Her younger brother always used to say that we've left behind the twentieth century and have stepped into the twenty first. We all live in the modern era, so why should we continue to dwell on things outdated?

'If that was the case, then why was I made to suffer? I too am part of this modern-day world; why was I abandoned then? Abba only educated his sons and helped them lead a successful life. Why did he not make me capable of earning my own livelihood and leading my life the way that I wanted to? Why was I condemned to the archaic world?'

As was obvious, the only response to all her angst was an all-encompassing deafening silence.

Her emotions had long gone cold. The Wasim of her dreams also had vanished into thin air. Once in a while, even when he did intrude upon her thoughts, she'd avoid him altogether showing her displeasure through her silences.

'You hurt me even in my dreams, Wasim,' she'd mutter to herself.

'My son has been craving for a new bike for the last three years. No one is bothered, neither his father nor your father. I know, he's our only son, but he is also the only son in-law of your father. He just paid pittance and relieved himself of all responsibility. What would my son do with all that? Eventually it's you only who'd be using them. The least that he could have done was to have gifted him something that he liked. At least something good would have come out of this wedding,' muttered Badi Ammi darkly as she sat on the bed chewing betel leaf. The whiff of intense grudge that she exuded through her nasty words reached the poor daughter in-law and turned icy cold as it hit her deathly silence.

Wasim came home in the afternoon for lunch. As she came out with his food, Ammi took the plate from her hands and said, 'You go and do your work. I'll serve him his lunch.'

For the past several days, both of them looked quite pleased with themselves. They spent long hours together discussing something furtively. Badi Ammi's face also appeared less tense these days.

Through the neighborhood women Amma got to know that Wasim was having an extramarital affair with another girl called Nusrat and spends his entire day lolling at her place. She was furious with them for spreading such nonsense about Wasim.

'Don't you women have any other work other than bad-mouthing my son in-law? How can you stoop so low?'

One of them retorted back, 'Don't tell us what's good or bad. You also know what a wastrel he is.'

Although Amma had managed to send the women away, but somewhere in the corner of her mind she too had a lurking suspicion.

And when she shared her concern with her husband that evening, he said,

'Whatever he is, he is after all our own blood, a part of our own family. I'm sure, he'd never go astray. You are worrying yourself unnecessarily and wrecking my nerves too. Get a grip on yourself and mind your own business. Look after your own house first.'

Badi Ammi had been away from the house since morning. She had left around nine without saying a word to anyone and had also taken her *burka* with her. As usual, Gudiya also had not asked her where she was going. It was nearly 2 o'clock in the afternoon and still there was no sign of her.

Gudiya washed her hands and readied herself to offer the afternoon *namaz*. Just as she was about to finish, the front door creaked and she had to get up in the middle of her prayers.

'It must be Badi Ammi,' she thought and got up to open the latch.

It was indeed her. She greeted her and turned back. But before she could take the next step, her eyes widened with shock. Wasim was right behind her. He was wearing a rose and jasmine garland round his neck and chewing betel leaf, laughing callously.

One by one everyone came in but Gudiya stood there shell-shocked.

She heard some indistinct voices coming from a distance. Badi Ammi went into her room and brought The Koran. She kept it on the head of the *burka*-clad woman and asked her to step in. A shadow glided past, leaving Gudiya behind. She stood there like a statue with a dazed look in her eyes as the door closed behind her.

No one even bothered to ask her what was wrong with her. She was deserted there, left alone.

Badi Ammi caressed the head of the *burka*-clad woman and blessed her wholeheartedly wishing that she may soon enjoy motherhood. She then took her into Wasim's room. And soon Wasim also followed her with a bag in his hands.

But Gudiya remained glued to the ground, unable to move. Life had come to a complete standstill for her. The fear that had been lurking in some corner of her mind had turned into a reality. It was staring in her face.

Badi Ammi came out of the room and closed the door behind her. Seeing Gudiya still standing at the same spot, she taunted, 'How long will you stand there like a statue? Won't you serve us any tea-coffee?'

The sarcasm in her voice was loud and clear, and there was absolutely no sign of any embarrassment or guilt on her face.

'Come on, now. You don't need to be so shocked. Go to the kitchen and start preparing for the evening meals. Make chicken biryani today,' saying this she went towards her room.

Gudiya simply stood there, not knowing where to go. The doors of her own room had been closed on her. She could hear the sounds of laughter coming from there. Soon the voices within her also grew louder and louder piercing her ears and heart.

When the news reached Gudiya's house, there was chaos everywhere. Amma began to howl at the top of her voice and her brothers were livid. Their anger was directed more towards their own father rather than towards Wasim.

Abba too was stunned. He got up from the bed only to sit down again, drained of all energy. His attempts at scripting his daughter's destiny had probably sapped his vigor or maybe his own sense of self-worth had shattered him completely.

His elder son, Kareem confronted him with arms folded. 'I'm sure you would be at peace with yourself now for having tied up Gudiya's future with a wastrel like Wasim! Aren't you pleased that you have written such a wonderful destiny for her?'

Abba was taken aback by his brazen outrage. His sons who had always been obedient and compliant, now were openly confronting him.

'Is she your sister alone? Is she no one to me? Am I not pained to see my own daughter's house broken to pieces?'

'If you really are pained, go and talk to your elder brother and his son,' Kareem raised his pitch louder.

Seeing his son's sternness, Abba could not sit there any longer. He took his shoulder cloth and left the house.

It was dark outside, but the darkness that had begun to seep into his very being was even murkier. The inner abyss kept growing deeper and deeper and he felt himself drowning in it. He had always presented himself as her guardian angel, but had he really been able to defend her interests or bestow his benefaction on her? He had no answer to that.

As he reached Wasim's house, his sister in-law welcomed him whole-heartedly and came and sat next to him on the chair. Then in a very casual manner she asked him, 'What brought you here today?'

'You know the reason quite well. I hadn't handed my daughter to you to be treated in such an unjust manner.'

'Unjust manner? Injustice has happened with us and with Wasim, Bhaijan, not with her. It's been three years since they got married, but she hasn't been able to give birth to a single child also. Does my son not have the right to further his own family line?'

'You have been advising people to lead their lives according to shariya laws. That is what we also have done. What wrong have we committed? Moreover, Wasim hasn't divorced your daughter that you walk in and demand an answer from us.'

Abba was struck dumb. He couldn't do anything but stare at the changing colors of his sister in-law's face. How far away has she gone? He was about to get up to leave when he saw Gudiya standing at the doorway with a cup of tea. She looked like a walking automaton.

Her face was pale and eyes expressionless. There was neither any sign of resentment, nor of relief upon seeing him. She did not seem to demand any answers from him either.

His little girl had grown into a woman. When and how did this transformation take place, he did not even realize. As he sat next to her, he found himself totally helpless. He could not look her into the eyes nor could he empathize with her grieving soul. Finding himself at a complete loss of words, he sneaked out sheepishly towards the doorway like a thief.

As he took the next step, Gudiya's expressionless eyes flashed before him and he couldn't see the stairs in front. He fell down. And that was his last fall. He was never able to recover from it again.

That very instant it dawned on him that he was no longer required to script Gudiya's destiny. That entitlement had been taken away from him by her husband. Wasim had now become his daughter's *rehnuma*, her custodian, her keeper, her guardian whereas he had been rendered useless.

And the soul parted from his mortal remains.

Gudiya did not shed a single tear at her father's demise. She recalled her Amma's words which said, 'Allah is there in the skies. Sitting from there he showers his benedictions and writes the destiny of all his people.'

'The apt place for a *rehnuma* is the skies only. They'd be able to write a better destiny from there,' Gudiya muttered to herself.

****

'Hashim Miya, Hashim Miya...Oh, here you are. I have been looking for you for so long. You don't seem to be listening. What's the matter? You look so lost?' handing him his cup of tea, Shahida Begum asked.

Hashim Miya indeed looked lost and dazed. He seemed to have emerged out, after having lived through a whole lifetime of experience. The remnants of Nazma's ravaged life were still visible in his eyes.

Wiping his eyes with his hands he said, 'No, I'm very much here only. I was thinking about Nazma.'

'Don't think about the past. Let bygones be bygones. Now she's happy staying alone, isn't it? Then why do you want to rake up old wounds again?'

Hashim and Shahida Begum had four children. Nida was younger to Taha by two years and Mannan was the youngest of them all.

Rehan, his eldest child was a couple of years older than Taha. He was the quiet one. In fact, he was nearly three and a half years old when he first learnt how to speak. He'd sit quietly and play with his toys. Many a times, one didn't even know he was there. Hashim Miya was very gregarious by nature, he loved it when there was mayhem in the house. He wanted that his house should reverberate with plenty of sounds, be it laughter or hullabaloo or howling, for that is what makes a home alive.

It was Taha who filled life into his house, the way that he had always wanted it.

Rehan always used to cling to his mother whereas Taha, on the other hand, used to make everyone eat out of her palms. Hashim Miya was on cloud nine when the first words that came out of his two-year-old daughter's tiny mouth were 'Abbu'. He was ecstatic and he showered all his love and affection on her.

He felt very proud of that fact and used to say to his wife, 'Did you see, the first words that children normally speak are "Ma", but my daughter spoke "Abbu". You can keep your son to yourself, for me my daughter is more than enough.'

It wasn't as if he had less affection for Rehan, and he also knew that he too loved him as much but it was always Taha who was more expressive about her feelings. She would always hover around him till as long as he was in the house. She'd sometimes show him her toys and sometimes pout complainingly and say, 'Look Abbu, my doll has stopped blinking her eyes.' And Hashim Miya would pamper her with a new doll.

Thus, both of them shared a special camaraderie with each other. With Taha around, Hashim felt as if his younger sister was with him. Together they'd sit in the verandah and gaze at the starry skies for hours. When the entire household was glued to the TV set, Taha would sit in her father's lap and play with stars and moon.

'Abbu, why is moon there?' Taha would ask him innocently.

'So that darkness is not deceived into believing that it can frighten anyone. God spread the moonlight to dispel darkness away.'

'Then there should be many moons. There are so many stars but only one moon…why?' Before she'd get an answer to her first question, her next one would be ready.

Hashim Miya would tell her indulgently, 'Millions of stars also cannot spread as much of light as one moon, that is why Allah only made one moon-like my daughter Taha.'

'Then Abbu, do I also sparkle like the moon…? Taha's eyes twinkled brightly as she shot another question.

Hashim Miya hugged her with affection and said, 'Yes, my moon. You are the brightest child. Whoever sees you, gets bedazzled.'

Little Taha barely understood the meaning of it all, but she swelled with pride.

Sitting in her father's lap, Taha found answers to all her queries. She felt alive and loved.

Hashim Miya was a senior officer in the State Electricity Board, so he did not face any financial difficulty in bringing up his four children. There was no dearth of finances. Moreover, both the husband and wife were well-read and responsible. They got their children educated in reputed English medium schools. Shahida Begum also had passed her Senior School so she too realized the importance of good education.

Under the strict guidance of their parents, the children also cleared their respective classes with flying colors. From their father, they inherited the knack of putting across their ideas in a straightforward and prudent manner. And from their mother they inherited a great dedication towards education. Shahida Begum herself was extremely fond of reading. Her almirah was full of books that ranged from Hindi and Urdu literature to the latest best-sellers. After finishing off all her household chores she'd retire to her room and indulge in her passion. Taha too, developed a keen interest in reading when she found herself surrounded by innumerable books.

By the time Taha reached the sixth standard, she had already started participating in the debate competitions. Her forthrightness and candor proved to be a great asset.

A day after the competitions, Hashim Miya knew that when he'd pick up the newspaper and turn to the local news section, he would find Taha striking a pose with the winner's trophy in her hands. And he would be invariably right.

'Taha, of St. Sophia School stood First in the State level Debate Competition...'

Hashim Miya would be on cloud nine on seeing his daughter's name in the headlines with her photograph below. In her white shirt and skirt with two plaits, he found her to be the most beautiful child in the entire world.

He'd collect all the newspapers of that day and show them off to his relatives and then he'd cut all those clippings and very proudly arrange them date-wise in a separate file. The cuttings kept growing and he soon found himself running short of pages.

It pleased Amma to see how much Hashim loved his daughter, but was wary too at the same time. Somewhere in the corner of her heart there lurked an unknown fear.

'It's not good to be so emotionally involved with daughters, Hashim.' She'd whisper gently.

Although Hashim was the complete opposite of his own father, but somewhere in him Amma could also see his father's reflection. She felt as if he was another *rehnuma* in making. She noticed his obsession towards cultivating and honing his daughter's destiny better. And that frightened her immensely leading her into seeking Allah's blessings for their wellbeing and safety.

One day Taha's maternal uncle came from Udaipur. He brought with him a beautiful cage full of multi-colored birds for children to play with. He reminded everyone of Mannan's visit to Udaipur and how every time he used to throw tantrums upon seeing his cage full of birds and pigeons on the terrace and pester him to get them for him also.

So, his Mamu decided to fulfill his wish that day.

Mannan was ecstatic with his new gift. He took it with him, climbed the stairs and went to the balcony where he put it down on an old broken table. Taha also followed close behind him.

'Why did you keep it here?'

'Mamu also keeps his cage in the balcony. It is big and looks good there, isn't it? Look, right now we have just two birds. When they'll give birth to more birds, we'll also have plenty of them. Then we'll buy a bigger cage for them,' Mannan said enthusiastically.

Taha scowled badly and went near the cage. She asked the birds, 'How do you feel trapped inside?'

'Don't be stupid. They can't listen to your talk, so how will they reply?' Mannan knocked her on her head.

'They have been put in a cage because they cannot speak. If they could, they'd be able to share their suffering.'

'Oh, they aren't humans that they'd feel bad for not getting the toys of their liking,' he tried to explain to his sister as they climbed downstairs.

'They don't want toys; they want open skies.'

'No, they just want something to eat and that they would get plenty in their cage.'

'Merely eating and drinking isn't life. Life is what one lives according to one's own free will,' Taha replied.

There was a sad look on Taha's face as she sat next to her Abbu in the evening.

Abbu caressed her head gently and asked, 'What happened to my little moon, why is it so sad?'

'Papa, the skies are so beautiful and vast. There is no wall or boundary in between. If anyone gets a chance to fly in these open skies, they wouldn't want to stay trapped behind the walls?'

'Yes dear, you are right.'

'Nobody would like to remain trapped behind the walls to merely satisfy their own hunger, Abbu?'

'Yes, dear. If they have wings to fly, they would hate to be trapped. The vast blue skies are their life. They'd only be alive if they fly unencumbered in these open skies.'

'Then why do we keep them in a cage?'

Hashim Miya understood very well what was bothering his daughter.

'Yes, it is wrong. Now go off to sleep. Tomorrow we'll see that these birds reach their homes in the high sky. Is that alright?'

Early next morning Taha completely forgot about the birds and left for her school. Her mind was occupied with the forthcoming essay competition that day. She was trying to memorize the points that she had scribbled in her rough note-book about 'whether there's life on the moon or not?' This time again she wanted to come first.

When she got down from the school rickshaw with bag on her shoulders, she had the certificate in her hands. Jumping with joy she went straight into Amma's room and said, 'Look, today again I stood first in the competition.'

'Wah! That's so wonderful. You are very talented. This has got your name also written in big letters.' Amma didn't know how to read, but she knew how to make her granddaughter happy. After showering her with praises, she handed over the certificate to her mother, who immediately kissed her on her forehead.

Amma really admired the way Shahida Begum used to encourage young Taha unlike her, who only used to push Nazma into household chores. Never once did she try to read her mind or peep into her heart.

She tried hard to forget the wrongs that they, as parents, had perpetrated towards their only daughter Gudiya a.k.a. Nazma. She still couldn't absolve herself of that guilt.

Taha finished her homework and waited for her Abbu to return back from work. She knew that if she opened the cage and released the birds without Abbu by her side, Mannan would pick up a huge fight with her.

Hashim Miya came back, changed his clothes and turned towards the staircase. Taha followed him and so did Mannan. He said to Mannan, 'Look son, aren't these two birds looking rather sad?'

'Yes Abbu, they are. But the birds that come to our courtyard keep chirping happily all the time.'

Abbu said, 'Yes, those birds are free to fly wherever they want to, that is why they sing happily. But if you put them in a cage, they would also stop chirping. Allah has provided them with vast limitless skies, they look good there only. I'm sure you'll also feel happy to see them flying.'

Then Abbu stepped ahead and released the pin of the lock and Taha set them free.

Taha did not like to see them behind bars, just as Hashim also did not like to see Taha silent. Taha had given the birds boundless skies to fly in, similarly Hashim had given Taha the freedom to live her life to the fullest.

Taha soared higher and higher under her father's patronage, achieving one milestone after another. He paved a path for her where there were no restrictions, no hurdles of any kind. He did not allow her to get cooped up in any enclosure that would clip her wings. She thanked the Almighty for having blessed her with such an understanding and caring father who protected her at every step.

'Hashim son, Taha is getting taller and her skirt is getting shorter. It doesn't look good, does it?'

Taha interrupted her in mid-sentence and said, 'Amma, you don't know, but this is how it is worn in our school. Skirts that go below the knees don't look smart.' She tried to explain.

'Don't teach me what's "smart", what's more important is propriety,' Amma also retorted back.

Hashim Miya also nudged in, 'Amma, grow up now. This is the twenty first century. Now look, there'll be approximately over a thousand girls in her school and everyone would be wearing the same type of clothes. Do you think they all would have compromised with their morality? Moreover, one cannot judge one's morality merely on the basis of their clothes.'

Amma fell silent. Her eyes glistened like those of a child. She knew very well that Hashim would always give a counter logic and silence her.

Taha finished off her school assignment and came on the terrace in the evening as usual. Karima was already there waiting for her. She was her childhood friend, who stayed next doors. There was a common wall that separated their houses. Both of them would perch on it and chatter away endlessly. Although they did not attend the same school, but both of them had become thick friends. There was a big gap in their upbringing and living styles, but it never came in between their friendship.

Karima was only allowed to complete her fifth standard from a *madarsa* near Ghatgate. After that she was never sent to any school. She was told that she had become a grown-up and wasn't allowed to even step out of the house.

Taha on the other hand, had always studied in the English medium schools right from the beginning and now she was in the tenth standard. The other difference was that Taha could go out in her frock or jeans whenever she wanted, but Karima was allowed to go out only on special occasions and that too after wearing a *burka.*

Karima's father did not like his daughter's friendship with Taha. He felt that she too would get spoilt. But hiding from everyone's gaze, Karima would quietly sneak to the terrace as soon as the clock struck five.

Taha would ask her, 'Don't you feel suffocated sitting inside the house the whole day? As for myself, I cannot sit at home even for a single day. It's so difficult to pass time specially when we have an off day at school.'

Karima would just laugh it away, saying, 'I've got used to it. I don't feel bad now. Everyone doesn't have a father like yours, that they'd hand over the freedom in a platter as if it were a chocolate.'

This used to make Taha swell with pride. She used to share all the details about her school life with her, she'd tell her about herself, about her friends. And Karima, on the other hand, would tell her about the different ways in which she cooked various curries, in which ones she put excess spices, for which ones she got praises from the family etc. This was what they generally talked about. Their talks were as different as their destinies were apart.

Karima had never been to a big school whereas Taha had never learnt how to cook the salan. Despite that they used to listen to each other's talks very intently.

Taha often shared her concerns about Karima with her father. She wanted her also to go to school like her and also to wear clothes of her own choice, like she did. Hashim Miya tried to explain to her that it was their family matter and was best left to them to handle it their way. He also added that probably her father must have already thought it through for the good of his own daughter.

'There is nothing better than freedom, Abbu. You also know that, isn't it? She is as much a live being as his sons. The sons keep loitering in the streets the entire day and she can't even go to school. Is that right?'

Hashim Miya was amused by the manner in which Taha advocated for women's rights but would get perturbed by her bluntness too. He did not want her to get entangled in any controversy with Karima's father or her brothers. She had always been outspoken even as a child or maybe he himself was responsible for making her the person that she had become.

He realized that there was a big disparity between the atmosphere at home in which he had brought up his children and that of Ghatgate neighborhood where they resided. The liberal upbringing that he had provided to his children, was looked down upon by the people there. And his children also did not much like their narrow-minded attitude and often found themselves at loggerheads with someone or the other.

Taha had created quite a furor at Karima's wedding also and for that Hashim Miya and his family had been bad-mouthed by many people.

As soon as Karima turned eighteen, her marriage was fixed up by her parents. Taha was very upset with her friend for not having resisted it and made her displeasure amply clear when she went to her house.

The marriage was solemnized at the close by *madarsa* and despite the difference of opinion, Taha tried her best to partake in the wedding festivities. All through the ceremony she sat next to her friend. And as soon as it got over, she along with her other friends and Karima's sisters went to the groom to tease him and have some innocent fun. But when she saw the bridegroom, she was appalled. Karima's groom was much older than her. The age gap between them must have been at least thirty odd years. He had a big flowing beard and his mouth was stained red with betel leaf that he was chewing.

Even in her wildest imagination, Taha couldn't believe that he would be the groom, her friend's life partner. But when Karima's sister addressed him as *dulha* bhai, Taha lost her temper and made her disapproval amply clear.

'You are the bridegroom! You've come here to marry or for *naat khwani*? For today at least, couldn't you have groomed yourself properly? At least that would have made you look a little more presentable while standing with Karima.'

Taha's words let loose a volley of frayed tempers and there was utter mayhem at the venue. The groom swallowed the betel leaf and its juice in one go, while Karima's sisters and cousins began to hurl abuses at Taha left, right and center.

'Who do you think you are! Having studied a few classes, you think you've become a star? Why must we endure your presence? Is this how you show your curtesy to the guests of honor, the bridegroom in your family?'

Within no time, the entire family of the groom gathered there.

When Taha's mother came to know about the ruckus that her daughter had created, she quickly went there and dragged her out of the crowd and brought her home. She then went back to apologize to the women there.

Taha's Abbu also had to plead for everyone's forgiveness.

Karima's father was livid with rage. He warned him in no unclear terms, 'You all look better in your own house. You should stay there only. You don't need to come at all and spoil our wedding festivities.'

Hashim Miya felt deeply insulted and humiliated. He came back and reprimanded Taha, 'Where was the need for this kind of brutal honesty, Taha? Aren't you aware of their narrow-minded attitude? What have you achieved by it all?

Let Karima marry whosoever they chose for her? Why are you so bothered?' Hashim continued to vent out his anger at Taha.

'Abbu, but what a mismatch it was? Didn't you notice it yourself? Why didn't her parents think about it before marrying her off to such an old man?'

'What concern is it of yours? Your Abbu-Ammi are there to take care of your wellbeing, aren't they? Isn't that enough?'

'No, that's not enough. It is not I alone but every girl deserves her freedom. They deserve to be free to live their life as they want to live. They at least should have the right to choose whom to marry and whom not to.

I cannot turn a blind eye to what's going on around me.'

And Hashim Miya was rendered speechless by his own daughter.

Since Taha wasn't at fault, Hashim Miya couldn't curb her spirited nature but at the same time he found the barbed comments of the people rather exasperating. Each day became a challenge for them to stay in the same locality. People also had begun questioning the kind of upbringing that he was providing to his children. He realized the futility of justifying his viewpoint to all and sundry and as such avoided all confrontation.

The area that they stayed in, was still under-developed and was at considerable odds from the bustling city-life of Jaipur, where everything was comparatively more advanced. Majority of the old houses in Jaipur had been converted into high-rise multistoried apartments with no dearth of shopping malls. The international chains from multiplexes to entertainment centers were all there. People had begun meeting at swanky coffee parlors instead of old tea-shacks.

Jaipur had also become a great education hub where students from all over India came for further studies. It had begun to get counted amongst one of the most progressive and beautiful cities of India. The big stars from the film industry also came for a sojourn there. People no longer found the hip modernity in the state-of-the-art colleges strange or out of place.

But it wasn't so for the people of Ghatgate, where Hashim Miya used to stay with his family. For them the environment in the city was too modern and fast-paced for their liking.

Ghatgate was a fairly huge neighborhood with not less than ten schools at least, but they were all up to the tenth standard only. Apart from that there was an Education Trust with a madrasa and a girl's college affiliated to it. But only those girls, whose parents understood the importance of education, were able to reach there.

Although there were separate education centers for girls, but the environment there wasn't any different from that of their homes. There were endless restrictions and dos and don'ts for them. They couldn't go anywhere without wearing their *burka.*

There wasn't any big college for boys either. As such, most of them did not study beyond their tenth or twelfth standard. They did not accord much importance to education probably because they had their ancestral occupation to fall back upon and carry it forward. People were generally engaged in the work of jewel-polishing to which women and children also contributed in their spare time. That helped them to substantiate the family income significantly.

Others owned small kiosks and shacks for non-vegetarian food and tandoor from which they were able to earn a decent livelihood. People from far and wide frequented this place to eat the mouth-watering non-veg cuisine, some of them would also get it packed and take it with them. The onus of running these kiosks depended largely upon the women folk who had already exhausted themselves with the jewel-polishing work.

Since people of this area had the means of livelihood already charted out for them, education did not mean the same thing as it did to Hashim Miya. Neither were they able to appreciate the fact that his children were well-read. It wasn't as if Hashim wanted any credit or acknowledgement from them, but somehow it became rather challenging for him to strike the right balance between the outer and the inner environment of the house. And knowing Taha's nature, he felt that it would be much better if they shifted elsewhere.

Thinking about all that Hashim Miya kept tossing and turning in his bed throughout the night when finally, Shahida Begum asked him, 'What happened? You look upset.'

'Oh, you haven't slept till now!' turning towards his wife he said.

'You've been a little lost since the evening. You did not even eat your food properly, what's the matter?' his wife probed.

'Yes, I am worried. I feel quite anxious about the widening chasm between the home and the outside world,' he replied.

'Are you upset with the storm that Taha raked up? She's still a child, doesn't understand what she has done.'

'No, no. I don't have any grouse against Taha. She said the right thing, but the people to whom she said, don't seem right. They don't understand and appreciate her feelings here. We have always taught her to be independent, and live her life as she pleases. Now she wants the same freedom for each and every girl. How can that be possible?'

'Yes, that's true. But what can we do about it?' Shahida Begum again asked him.

'I'm thinking of changing our residence. Let us shift to a better locality where our children would get a more congenial atmosphere. Look at Mannan…he also keeps getting into fights with someone or the other all the time.'

'But that's not so easy. How would we be able to live without our entire family if we leave this house behind? And moreover, Amma would never agree to it.'

'She would. Let me talk to Kareem Bhai tomorrow. He, anyways, was finding it difficult to accommodate his growing family in his small house. He had expressed keenness towards taking this portion in the past.'

'But if he comes to know that we intend to leave this place and move out, he would also get upset.' Shahida Begum tried to reason out.

'No, he is not like that. If I tell him that we want to move out because of Taha, then he also wouldn't mind. He, in fact, would be quite pleased. When Nazma was young, he often used to tell Abba that he shouldn't allow himself to be influenced by the opinions of his relatives. He never wanted them to dictate our lives, but Abba refused to listen to him. Since then, there has been no love-lost between them, but because he was born and brought up here, he has become very attached to this place. He has spent his entire life here after all.'

Early next morning, after finishing off his breakfast, Hashim Miya left for his brother's place.

His brother heard the entire incident and said, 'If you also yield to them out of fear, who would change their mentality? Seeing the atmosphere of your house, a couple of relatives might be persuaded to change their outlook and decide not to curb their daughters within the four walls of their houses.'

'No, bhaijan, I don't know whether that would ever happen or not but it would definitely lead to lot of bad blood. All these things have an adverse effect on the children's education too. It would be better for us to shift to another place altogether.'

'I don't have any problem, but you need to make Amma understand all this. If she wants, she can stay with us. It won't be easy for her to leave all this and go away,' his elder brother said.

'Yes, but Amma would go with us. We have got so used to her staying together that we can't imagine going without her. We also wouldn't like it without her,' Hashim Miya said.

'Yes, that's true. Even we don't like it without her. But she doesn't want to stay with me even till this day. She still holds me responsible for Abba's death.'

'Bhai, it was nobody's fault. That was Allah's wish. Take it off your chest and stop blaming yourself for what happened years ago.'

'Any way, let's leave all that. Tell me, what have you thought? Where do you intend to take up this new place? You'd invite us to your new bungalow, won't you?' Kareem tried to pull his leg.

'One of the assistant engineers from my office stays in Pratap Nagar area. He says that area is quite peaceful. Although there aren't too many houses and the place is still developing, but people like staying there.

I think it would be a good idea to buy a plot of land and build a house there. The concept of selling ready-to-move-in houses hasn't come up as yet. And you know, how difficult it is to find a good house in the city these days. So, I think I should settle for it.'

'But just be careful, think over it thoroughly before you commit yourself. The distance from here would be quite a lot. It shouldn't happen that later you find it cumbersome to commute from that far,' his elder brother tried to caution him.

'What kind of problems? There are plenty of buses available from there. My boss's wife measures the entire city by bus only.' And both the brothers burst out laughing.

Hashim Miya finished his tea and left for his home.

Shahida begum was engrossed in folding the clothes and putting them in the almirah, when a card popped out and fell on the floor.

'Oh, this looks like a birthday card. Probably one of her friends must have given it to Taha on her birthday, a couple of days back.' Without giving it much thought, she picked it up and put it back from where it had fallen and closed the door.

Then for no reason at all, she reopened the almirah and took the card out. It read, 'My sweetheart Tahu, wish you a very happy birthday, yours I will be yours…'

Her heart missed a beat. She read and re-read it over and over again and found that the sender hadn't written his/her name on it.

'I'm unnecessarily getting all worked up, all her friends write it this way only. Many a times, when they bring any gift, they just scribble "sweetheart" and "love you" on it...'

'Oh, these girls! They've become completely westernized. The kind of messages that they exchange can put anyone to shame. I'm sure it must be one of her friends playing a prank on her. That is why she deliberately did not write her name.'

However hard she tried to reason it out with herself, she was assailed by a nagging suspicion, 'A growing girl's mother, however modern she might be, can never take refuge behind the cloak of modernity and remain oblivious to this kind of anxiety.'

'This foolish girl thinks that she knows everything. So, what if she has studied a few classes? Has she has become an expert? She's too young and inexperienced to gauge the real intents of people. The only thing she knows is how to fight. And, who would fall for such an aggressive girl like her!'

'Boys generally like compliant girls who can flatter their huge egos and do their every bidding.'

'And the only thing that Taha is capable of, is denting male egos.'

Shahida Begum reflected upon her daughter's nature and chuckled.

Trying to divert her wayward thoughts, she sat on the bed with her books. Reading books of literature was her favorite pass time and she loved indulging herself in it whenever she was all alone.

Taha also used to keep in mind her fondness for books. In her school library, she'd often go to the Hindi Literature section and if she happened to lay her hands on the works of Amrita Pritam, Sharat Chandra, she'd get them issued for her. Before her mother was able to finish reading one book, she'd bring another one for her.

Sometimes she would also read them herself, but often lacked patience when it came to heavy novels. She'd read a few pages from the beginning, few from the middle and quickly reach the climax.

Taha wasn't like other girls of her age. She wasn't much interested in getting dressed or applying make-up or wearing jewelry. She'd wear anything that came in her hands and wouldn't think twice about attending the wedding functions also in plain ordinary clothes. Abbu would laugh at this habit of hers and say, 'It's good, isn't it? She's saving me a lot of expenses.'

Taha had written her standard twelfth examination and was desperately waiting for the results to be declared. She was under a lot of stress as she sat in the courtyard gazing at the moon when her Abbu came in.

'What's the matter? You didn't even eat your meals properly?'

'Yes Abbu, I'm worried about my results. If I don't score well in my senior secondary exams, I won't be able to secure a seat in any of the good colleges.'

'So, how does that matter? There are so many private colleges these days. You give donation and take admission. You don't have to worry at all. I'll take care of everything.' Hashim Miya tried to reassure his daughter.

'No, Abbu. As far as the private colleges are concerned anyone and everyone can get admission, but I'd like to join the University only. And you know, to be a 'pass out' from Maharani College has a different charm altogether.'

'It is every girl's dream to go there, but only the top creamy layer are able to make it. And it would be such an honor to be a part of the University.'

Taha shared her deep-rooted desire with her father.

'Yes, so what? You have always secured more than 85 percent marks in your examinations. And it isn't less by any standards that you'd face problems with your admissions.' Hashim Miya patted her back and tried to pep her.

'It's not enough, Abbu. Haven't you seen that every year the merit list goes above 90 percent? And this year it's the Board Exams for me, God knows what would happen if I score less than 85 percent. Then my dream would remain a dream forever.'

'No, it won't happen. It has never happened and will never happen that you'd fall short of expectations, Taha,' Abbu said.

Mannan stuck out his tongue and teased her, 'That you'd get to know only tomorrow morning.'

'And yes, if Taha *Baji* is unable to get admission in the University, then definitely teach her how to make good salan,' turning towards his mother he tried to pull his sister's leg.

Amma slapped him lightly and said, 'It won't happen. She'd surely get admission.'

But Taha, who was already quite tense, lost her cool and shouted at him, 'You only like girls who stay at home and cook delicious dishes.

Even the Kallu restauranter can cook good salan, so why don't you go and become his brother?"

Everyone burst out laughing at Taha's comment and began teasing Mannan. 'From tomorrow onwards you start calling him "*baji*" only.'

Mannan glared menacingly at them with his big round eyes.

Taha woke up very early next morning. It was only 5 o'clock. She couldn't go back to sleep again So she began to wait anxiously for the newspaper man to deliver the paper.

She sought Allah's blessings, and prayed for a good result and avowed to offer a floral tribute at the altar of Jiauddin sahib's dargah if she came out with flying colors. Although she was a modern girl who belonged to the 21st century, but she had deep faith in Allah and his prophets and was quite particular about offering *namaz* on time and paying her obeisance to the Almighty.

She turned towards her mother and found that she too was awake.

'Ammi, do you have to get up early today?'

'No, I too couldn't sleep.'

So, both of them got out of their beds, freshened up and offered the prayers. Then they sat down with a cup of steaming tea in their hands, 'Ammi, it doesn't make much sense to wait for the newspaper because it only gives the division. To know the exact percentage, we would have to wait for the marksheets.'

'Then why are you worrying so much? You didn't even sleep properly? Come on, do one thing, just go off to sleep again. And don't be in any hurry to get up.'

'No, I don't feel like sleeping. Ammi, I think I'll opt for Humanities for my graduation.'

'Eh, what happened? You've been studying science subjects till now, what makes you change your mind?'

'That's exactly what I'm trying to tell you. You know I like experimenting with newer things.'

'These so-called experimentations of yours might jeopardize your studies. Your marks could be badly affected.'

'No, nothing of that sort would happen. You wait and watch, I'll score good marks there as well,' oozing plenty of confidence, Taha assured her mother.

'But what will you achieve by changing your stream? Give me one good reason. If you complete your graduation and post-graduation in science, it's going to be very beneficial for you. After your M. Sc., you can go for a lectureship also. Don't you see there's so much more scope and options after a degree in Science?'

Her mother tried to drive some sense into her.

'That's true, but I don't like to follow the trodden path. I want to do something different.'

'Hmm…What is so unique that you'd achieve with a B.A.? Do you want to go in for a degree in Home Science?' Ammi teased her.

'No, Ammi, that I would learn anyways. You know, I want something different…' Taha tried to show off her style in front of her mother.

'Oh, something different? That's exactly what I'm asking you. What is it that you want to do differently?'

'I only know one thing right now. That I'll carve out a future for myself but that wouldn't be in science.'

'Has the newspaper man come?' Hashim Miya yawned loudly as he came out of his room.

'So, which sweets do you want me to get today? It will be better if you tell me in advance only.' Abbu asked her lightheartedly trying to ease off some tension.

'Abbu, we have planned a get-together in the evening today.'

'That's great, where is it?' Abbu teased Taha.

'No, you don't have to come. You just give me the money, then your role is over.'

'Oh, how nice! We foot the bills and we are the ones not invited. That's so kind of you, my little one.'

'Oh Abbu, I'll party with you at home with yummy rasagullas,' licking her lips Taha said.

The newspaperman threw the paper from the gate in such a manner that it fell straight into the courtyard.

'Here comes the paper and with that comes Tahu's result too.'

The wait for the newspaper was a mere formality. Everyone knew that her roll number would be in the column of all first divisioners and it was. Ammi kissed Taha's forehead and blessed her wholeheartedly saying,

'You've shown to the world that daughters also can bring a lot of glory to their fathers. Hashim gave you wings to fly and you've emerged true to his expectations. We are extremely proud of you, my dear.'

Hashim Miya too was ecstatic, he was happy with the fact that his upbringing had borne fruit.

The entire day just flew past with friends and relatives dropping in to congratulate Taha. The elder *Bhabhi's* sister also came, 'Heartiest congratulations Shahida, your daughter has made you proud,' she said.

'Yes, it's all because of Allah grace, it is he who rewards all hard work.'

'That's fine. But now start thinking about her marriage. Look at her, she isn't a child any longer.'

'Oh no, not at all, not right now. This is the time for her to enjoy and have fun.'

'Arre wah! Can't you see how fast she's growing? The girls of her age have already become mothers.'

Then she paused for a second and continued, 'If you agree, we can talk about my elder son. He has also passed his twelfth standard. He goes to a computer center and takes classes there. Taha would be very happy with him.'

Her keenness for this alliance came out loud and clear.

'No, no. We haven't thought about it right now. Let her complete her studies, then we'll think about these things,' said Shahida Begum trying to conceal her exasperation.

'It isn't very often that you get such good matches and that too sitting at home only. And just think, your daughter has already completed her twelfth and you know it very well that you wouldn't get a better qualified match than my son amongst all our relatives.'

Before Shahida Begum could retort, Amma's voice came from behind, 'So, are we dependent on your son?'

Realizing that things were getting out of control, *Bhabhi's* elder sister thought it was better to say goodbye and leave.

Shahida Begum rarely paid much attention to what people said, but once in a while their stray jibes about her daughter's budding youth, did rankle her. Why can't they refrain themselves from giving unsolicited advice?

She shared her dilemma with her husband in the evening.

'Why do you pay attention to all that nonsense? You get perturbed yourself and then you pass it all to me. Now let me sleep. I have to get up early morning tomorrow and find out about the last date of filling admission forms for Maharani College and then deposit the fees too. Right now, our only concern should be Taha's happiness. Let us focus on that rather than what people say.'

'Here take these sweets, Shahida Begum and serve it to everyone.'

'I have some good news. The land deal has been finalized with full payment done. We now have the registration papers of the property in our hands.'

Amma said, 'Oh, that's excellent. The more properties we have, the better it is, they'd come handy when both the sons grow up.'

'We'll think about the sons later, first let's fix up a place for staying.'

'A place to stay? What's wrong with this one? You are staying comfortably here, isn't it?'

'Hmm…Yes, quite comfortable, but I'm looking for a greater comfort now.'

'What more do you want, Miya?'

'A big bungalow, a car and a serene setting, far away from all the relatives. Now soon we'd go to our new house.'

'Which new house? What are you talking about? Where are we

going?'

'Look Amma, we now need a bigger place to stay. Here we run short of space. Whenever any guests come from outside, we don't have any place to accommodate them. And it gets embarrassing many a times, if there's an extra person at home. We have no place here. So, I'm planning to construct a big bungalow on the land that we've just bought.'

'I don't see any problem with this house, it's quite sufficient us.'

'Yes, but it's rather small.'

'So, how does it matter? We are closer to our people and are staying in our own ancestral house, that's more than enough.

It's your friends who must have brain-washed you, isn't it? They themselves have shifted to remote locations and now they want you also to do the same. I know that Surendra Singh, he must have prevailed upon you to shift out, isn't it?'

Amma got all worked-up.

'What will anyone teach me Amma? Am I a small child? I have already decided, we are getting a new house constructed in Pratap Nagar and my decision is final.'

'If you have already taken a decision, then why are you asking me? You are free to do what you want to do, but I'm going to stay here only.'

Hashim Miya knew that outwardly Amma would rave and rant but in her heart, she would always be with him only.

This time also she won't refuse. Although initially she'd feel bad leaving her old ancestral home, but would eventually give in.

Taha's marksheet also came and so did the college admission form. This time she had scored 89 percent marks, but was still under tremendous stress because the percentages in the merit-list were touching the skies.

Expressing her angst, she said to Abbu, 'Every year, during the admission days, the newspapers carry these huge headlines that the merit in this particular subject has crossed 90 percent and in that 95 percent. It seems Rajasthan University has become another Delhi University, where you must score a minimum of 90 percent marks if you want admission.'

'It would be difficult to secure admission even if you get 90 percent, dear. For D.U. you require more than 98 percent,' he corrected his daughter.

'Whatever it is, Abbu, it is really mindboggling, there is tremendous pressure on students to score well these days. Why do students study so much that they push the merit list to such unimaginable heights that they themselves end up getting stumped by it?'

'Don't take any stress, Taha. You would get admission.'

The construction of their new house on the 200 sq. yard plot got underway as soon as the concerned authorities approved the design. There was no dearth of finances since Hashim had a decent well-paying job. Moreover, his elder brother had purchased their ancestral house at the market rate.

Taha had secured admission in her favorite Maharani College and was extremely happy. Hashim Miya also breathed a sigh of relief for he knew that his daughter would have got badly disheartened otherwise.

The academic session was to start from 10th July. The very prospect of going to the college with both her close friends excited Taha. She along with them got busy with the preparations. They indulged themselves in a lot of shopping because they knew that in college, they'd no longer be required to wear uniforms.

'Eh, how's my new hair-cut?' Taha undid the ribbon and sought the approval of her brother and sister.

Nida chirped, 'Wow *Baji*! it is looking very good.' But Rehan and Mannan glanced at each other and started giggling.

'Are you going for a fashion parade or for studies?' Rehan chuckled,

'It's no use talking to the two of you. Is there any problem in grooming yourself well? The girls that come there are very chic. I don't want to look like a fool in front of them,' Taha retorted loudly.

'Where's the question of "looking like a fool", that you already are!' Mannan winked at Rehan and both burst out laughing.

Nida tried to salvage the situation, '*Baji*, let go off these boys, they are silly. Believe me, you look very smart in this new hair-cut.'

And finally, the day arrived when Taha put her first step inside the college. She got down from the bus at the Ajmeri gate stop and walked towards the entrance where her friends, Meera and Shahna were waiting for her. There were two note-books in her hands.

She knew that the campus was beautiful. Today it was unusually more crowded than normal days. The verandahs were brimming with students and so were the lawns where the girls had formed their own groups. Some of them sat on the steps of the building itself chatting excitedly. The parking area also looked quite full. It appeared as if there was a gala all-girls fair going on, wherein had descended the glamour of the entire town. Taha herself looked pretty in pink kurta and white churidar pajamas and the compliments and appreciative glances that she received from her friends further boosted her confidence.

The most spectacular feature about that first day was the trendy outfits that were seen all around. The girls sported their own unique style, wearing different hues. Although jeans and shorts were the basic college gear, but the tees and shirts looked quite hip and happening too. From the kohl-lined eyes and stilettoes, one could easily guess the latest trend in the world of fashion.

Taha liked the color of somebody's dress and the shade of somebody's lip-gloss. When her excitement began to wane a little, she decided to look out for her classes. She asked a man, 'Where are the classes for the first years?' He was most likely the office peon.

Pointing towards a block, he began to chuckle, 'Who asks for classes on the first day?'

Meera said, 'We don't want to know, but what can we do? This studious friend of ours doesn't want to miss her classes even on the first day.' She then pointed towards Taha and they all burst out laughing.

It was nearly two o'clock and they were all hungry. 'Let's go home,' one of them said.

Shahna said, 'But why do we need to go home for food? Let's go to the canteen.'

'No, we'll go there on some other day. Let's go home now. I'm quite bored.'

'My dear friend, it's you who are a bore. Today's our first day in college and don't you think it would be advantageous for us to acquaint ourselves with other freshers and seniors? 'Shahna said.

'Oh, that we'll do later,' saying this Taha got up and holding her friends' hands, she pulled them up as well.

The three of them came out of the college and waited for the bus to come.

Right across the street, was the main entrance of Maharaja College, where stood several groups of boys. That's where she saw him for the first time, probably waiting for someone. He must have been twenty-one or twenty-two years in age, with fair complexion and brown hair, looking quite handsome in blue jeans and white t-shirt.

Taha felt his eyes on her. She felt a little unnerved at his behavior and averted her face. Then turning towards Shahna, she said, 'Let's move a little further away and wait for the bus.'

Meera said, 'Now what's the problem in waiting here, buddy? Enough of your attitude please?'

Without bothering to reply, Taha moved ahead a little. Her friends also had to move with her.

Taha still felt that boy's eyes following her.

Shahna too noticed the boy across the street and waving her hands at him, shouted loudly, 'Bhaijan, Bhaijan...'

Since he too was looking towards them, it wasn't difficult for Shahna to catch his attention. He immediately came over on his bike.

'Bye-bye girls, you both can find your way home. I'm leaving with Zeeshan Bhaijan,' Shahna said as she took a few steps ahead.

He stopped his bike right behind Taha, but she felt too nervous to turn back and look at him. He honked loudly and whizzed past her in full speed leaving behind a lingering fragrance that made Taha's heart skip a beat.

When she boarded the bus to go home, she found herself repeating over and over again, 'Um...Zeeshan..., I think that is how Shahna had addressed him.'

From that day onwards, their eyes met every day as they entered or exited their respective colleges. He would be seen standing right in front of his college gate. Taha tried her best not to glance that way but her eyes would invariably turn towards him and when she found him staring back at her, mortified she would immediately drop her gaze. She didn't know whether he sat there the entire day or whether he knew about her college timings. She found his gaze constantly on her. She would often turn around to see whether he was actually looking at her or at someone else. May be his eyes were following someone else but she, like a fool, might be thinking that he was interested in her.

She found herself thinking about him all the time, whether at home, or while making her notes. Howsoever hard she tried, she couldn't free herself from dreaming about him. So much so, that before going to college, she had even begun spending hours in front of the dressing mirror. She wanted to look her best for him. She'd keep trying her dresses one after another and it would take her ages to select the one that she'd want to wear that day.

Taha was already blessed with a fair complexion and big beautiful eyes, pink lips that resembled rose-petals, long jet-black hair and excellent figure. Her tall beaming persona and poise invariably left the people around speechless. And on top of all this, her face had now begun to glow.

As someone had rightly said, love adds a divine radiance and charm to youth, when reciprocated in equal measure.

She wasn't like other girls of her age. Instead of the usual feminine grace, there was a trace of arrogance in her gait. But what distinguished her from others was the gravity on her face.

Her friends as well as her teachers had high regard for her.

As she entered her college, she looked towards the gates of Maharaja college to catch one glimpse of him. He wasn't there. As she reached the main building, she turned back once again. He was still not there. That day he was nowhere to be seen.

Next day when she found him standing at his usual place, her happiness knew no bounds. She smiled at him. He too smiled back. This exchange of smiles made her heart go topsy-turvy and she quickly disappeared inside her college.

She was lost in her own world the entire day, completely unaware about what was going on around her. The classes also went off smoothly.

She did not bump into anyone while passing through the verandah nor had to face Meera's stray remarks about her unusual behavior.

'What's the matter? You are in a very chirpy mood today. Have you won any lottery?' Asked Meera as she couldn't contain herself any longer.

'What lottery! I'm like this every day. What do you people think…' Taha replied.

'No, buddy, who would know you better than us? You aren't your usual self today. You look different.' Meera tried to probe.

'Don't even ask, how we feel right now…,' Shahna also began pull her leg.

It had been now four months since the construction of their new house had started. It was almost ready. The only thing that was left was the finishing work.

'It's good that there is a park opposite,' said Shahida Begum happily.

'Yes, both of us would go there for our morning walks,' Hashim Miya teased her.

'Oh my God! You just need an opportunity to rib me. I was talking about Amma. She is also thoroughly bored of staying in closed houses.'

Even before shifting there, everyone had already chosen the rooms that they'd occupy. They gave their color preference for the walls and also shared a list of the things that they wanted for their rooms. Abbu agreed to everything, but refused the demand for separate color T.V. sets in every room. He said with an air of finality that the T.V. would be installed in the hall and that they all would have to manage with one set only. Everyone knew that it would be impossible to do that because the control would forever be in the hands of Amma alone as it used to be in their old house. She'd either be viewing some horror show or some such serials like "Balika Vadhu" etc., the entire day. In the afternoons, she loved to watch some cookery show with which she had absolutely no connect. In their house it was mostly nonvegetarian food that used to get cooked and she watched all the vegetarian recipes. It was from these shows that she had picked up words like, olive oil, beans, corn flour etc.

Her grandchildren used to plead with her, humor her, use all kinds of tactics, but it was impossible to take the remote-control from her old wrinkled hands. And if by chance her favorite film "Suryavansham" was being screened by any of the channels, she wouldn't budge or let anyone disturb her.

The children too had devised a way out of this situation. They prevailed upon their father to not put Amma's bed in the hall. That would enable them to handle the remote and watch programs of their interest.

Taha looked forward to their shifting to Pratap Nagar for she knew that once they did, she'd get a new scooty. But Shahna cautioned her saying, 'It's not a small distance to travel by a two-wheeler. You'd feel exhausted by the time you reach college.'

'Don't be silly. I'd be driving it and not carrying it on my shoulders.'

'Oh God! You and your sense of humor. No one can match that.'

'Yes, no one can match me,' replied Taha with full confidence.

'Yes, that's what I'm saying…'

'What's the matter? What is it that you want to say?'

'Just that he is completely besotted by you.'

'Who?'

'He, who brings a smile on your face as soon as you enter college.'

Taha's face grew crimson but she tried to conceal her feelings and asked, 'Whom are you talking about?'

'Now don't play the innocent with me. God has given me two eyes that see and one brain that can put two and two together.'

'Come on, don't talk in riddles, tell me whom are you talking about?' asked Taha pulling at her braid.

'Now that you pulled my hair, I won't tell you anything. Just go away.'

'Alright, suit yourself. I'm not dying to know.'

'Oh really? It's written all over your face, however hard you may try to conceal your feelings.'

'What's written on my face?'

'That you've begun to pine for something.'

'That's nonsense!'

'Oh, so now my talks are 'nonsense' to you!'

'Alright forget it,' Shahna conceded. She then took out one envelope from her bag and put it in front of Taha.

Taha's heart did a somersault. She quickly picked it up and put it in her bag.

When she was all alone in the house, she took it out from her bag. Her fingers quivered and her heartbeats increased as she opened it. There was a small red heart-shaped card inside. In it was written a small couplet in English. The sender hadn't put Taha's name on the card, neither did he put his. Towards the end, was written, "yours I will be yours…"

She read and re-read it over and over again trying to recall where else had she seen those words.

'Oh yes, now I remember. Somebody had put a similar card inside my school bag on my birthday also. I still don't know who did that till this day.'

She opened her almirah and rummaged through her clothes. There it was, stuck to the back of the shelf. She took it out and stuffed the clothes back.

The wordings and the handwriting were ditto…exactly same, with "yours I will be yours…" written in the end.

She was perplexed. How did Zeeshan's card come into her bag!

Next day, she confronted Shahna and tugged at her long braid. That was what she used to do whenever she wanted to teach her a lesson.

'Let go off my hair, otherwise you won't hear anything from me.' Shahna warned her.

Taha let go off her hair and clutched her arm instead.

Shahna said, 'Remember, the day you had come to my house to take the biology book…'

'Yes, so…'

'That day Zeeshan Bhai was sitting in the living room.'

'Alright, I did not notice.'

'So what? He noticed you.'

'Okay, then?'

'Then it so happened, that he got completely smitten by you. You have taken his heart hostage.

Poor wretched soul has absolutely no idea what's he getting into. He has fallen for a haughty girl like you.'

'Eh, don't be silly.'

'Yes, he has fallen head over heels in love with you and is spending many a sleepless night. He lies awake for hours thinking about you. He's gone insane.'

'Forget this love sonnet, tell me, how did the card reach my bag?'

'Hmm, it's these hands of mine which are culprits. I was helpless before my cousin's insistence.'

'And when I had asked you about it, you played the innocent with me?'

'I was scared. And madam, who would have guts enough to hand over love-letters to a snooty girl like you?'

Taha became a little serious then and asked, 'And what does this cousin of yours do?'

'Love. These days, he's only engrossed in love.'

'You wouldn't improve your ways, would you? Tell me the truth, please.'

'He's also studying. He studies in Maharaja College which is right opposite our college. And he's a final year student of B.A. Honors.

His brother has a house on M.D. Road and his father has a Men's-wear Showroom in Ganpati Plaza.'

'Alright, and who else is there in his family?'

'Does it mean that you also feel equally inclined to tie the knot? He's got one elder sister who is already married and a brother, Kamran. Zeeshan is the youngest of all his three siblings.'

In the meantime, the construction of their house got over and Taha decided to take one week off from her college.

Amma was sad for she didn't want to leave her old house and shift to a new place altogether. Nor did she want to stay without Hashim Miya as in all these years she had become quite fond of her four grand-children.

Besides, Shahida Begum's soft and compliant nature was another factor that tied her to the family. She admired her resilience and understanding, which she realized, comes only with good education.

'How wrong were we to believe that education makes women haughty and that girls who go to schools and colleges become misfits in their *sasural* after marriage. Shahida has removed all those misconceptions and transformed my way of thinking.'

And she blessed her kind, well-read daughter in-law from the bottom of her heart.

It wasn't just Amma alone but every member of the household had tears in their eyes as they left their old house behind.

Their new house was indeed grand. The ambience was lovely with plenty of greenery and wide-open roads. For Hashim Miya's family, who had spent their entire life cooped up in narrow by-lanes, this openness brought alive the child within. It was as if they were back in their younger days. Wide open roads, huge sprawling bungalows with a few apartments in between, the lush greens of park in the front and the foliage-caressed breeze that blew softly through those tall trees.

Even the breeze had ample space to move around as compared to the Ghatgate area where they used to reside earlier. There, even if one climbed on to the third floor, they'd not feel a single whiff of breeze as it got obstructed by the tall houses. The lanes too were so narrow that three-four people also could not pass without colliding with each other.

For Taha also it was quite convenient to commute to her college by scooty. But the flip side of it was that she could not see Zeeshan upon her arrival because she had to necessarily go to the parking lot first to park her vehicle. But she devised a way-out of this. She began to take a detour around the park in front of her college gate before proceeding towards her classrooms. That way she could see him standing right there at the entrance of his college every day.

One day, as she was about to leave for home, her friend, Shahna accompanied her to the parking lot and handed over an envelope. This time, there was a letter inside instead of a card. It read,

'Dearest Taha,

When you take leave from college even for a single day, I find it extremely difficult to wade through the entire day. But how does it matter to you? You are so busy enjoying your life. You don't even realize the depth of my anguish. Do you?'

As soon as Taha read his letter, she became equally restless and wanted to confide in him her own agony when she's not able to see him even for a day.

'He has asked me to give his message. He wants to meet you tomorrow at all cost....'

'No buddy, I won't be able to go.'

'Why not? What's the big issue, Taha? You simply have to go and talk to him. He is not asking you to elope with him that you are getting all flustered.

You can scare the hell out of ten boys without batting an eyelid but when it comes to love, you develop cold feet. This won't do. My brother is a decent soul. You have to meet him tomorrow for sure.'

'How will we meet and where?'

'In Ram Niwas gardens, where else.'

Taha felt extremely nervous. She desperately tried to calm down her racing heartbeats as she selected her favorite blue kurta and the matching combination of pink salwar-dupatta to go with it.

When she reached the gardens, Shahna and Zeeshan were already there. Taha's eyes refused to meet his as she stood frozen in her tracks, completely tongue-tied. There was an awkward silence amongst the three of them for a few seconds. Shahna discreetly left them both together with the pretext of buying some popcorn.

Indicating towards a near-by bench, Zeeshan requested Taha to sit. And as soon as they seated themselves, he took her hands in his. Taha felt her hands quiver, but she made no attempts to extricate them from his grasp. And Zeeshan also continued to hold them till the quivering subsided.

Taha found it difficult to breathe. She just sat there with her head bent, unable to lift her eyes before him. All these months they had been seeing each other from afar. She had always wanted to take a closer look at him. And now, when that opportunity presented itself to her, her own eyes refused to provide her that gratification.

Amidst all the pleasures and aches and labored breathings of their new found feelings, they were still holding each other's hands when Zeeshan broke the silence and asked her, 'How do you feel? Do you also reciprocate my love?'

Taha couldn't utter a single word. If only she could have reined her galloping heartbeats. Zeeshan again said, 'I never imagined that you'd be so shy.'

Taha, who a moment ago, was so coy, suddenly burst out laughing. She countered, 'Why? Can't I be shy? Am I not a girl?'

'Oh yes, that you are. But you aren't any girl. You are special. Anyone who sees you once, would lose his heart to you.'

The passion in Zeeshan's voice softened her heart and like a perennial rivulet she began to surge ahead towards an unknown journey. There was nothing to thwart her flow, no boulders, no restraints, nothing whatsoever.

Their silences had found words and they began to chat like old friends. They chatted about their childhood times, their friends, their families and their destinies together.

The branches of the trees, that were at the mercy of the hot afternoon sun, caught the stray sprightly breeze and began to sway gently, providing respite to the hearts that were in love. The birds too added to the background music with their sweet chirpings. Amidst all these bounties of nature, there was someone who was getting fidgety.

Shahna stood behind them with folded arms.

'Come on, let's go now. You've been going on endlessly. Will you people leave only after the family planning is complete? No one is bothered about me. I've been loitering around for nearly two hours now.'

Taha felt mortified as she tried to extricate her hand from his clasp, but Zeeshan was in no mood to let it go.

Shahna's light-hearted teasing made them get up from the bench. Taha was on cloud nine as she walked hand-in-hand with Zeeshan, experiencing the first stirrings of new sensations within her. She visualized him as her life-companion. It wasn't the flowers, but the cascading autumn leaves that lay strewn in their path, which added to the magic and made it even more special.

Soon the two began to meet each other regularly, sometimes in the gardens and sometimes in the coffee shops. At times, Zeeshan would reach G.T. to meet Taha. The yearning for togetherness grew stronger by the day. Their love blossomed and the next three years flew past in a jiffy.

Taha was quite confident that Abbu wouldn't turn down the proposal whenever Zeeshan's family came to their house to ask for her hand in marriage, but at the same time there lurked an unknown fear in some corner of her mind too.

Zeeshan completed his studies and began to work with his father and brother in the show-room. Taha also, on the other hand, finished her graduation with flying colors maintaining her previous record of eighty-five percent. She had not let her feelings affect her studies.

And once Taha's studies got over, her passion found new wings. She decided to pursue post-graduation in Journalism and took admission in Rajasthan university. She had confided in her father about her desire to be a journalist. Her family also was pleased with the fact that she was charting the course of her own destiny and supported her wholeheartedly in all her endeavors.

But, Zeeshan wasn't too happy with her decision and made his displeasure amply clear. He said, 'Why do you want to go in for more studies? What would you do after becoming a journalist? I have enough and more in my house. You won't find anything lacking there that you'd be forced to work?'

'Is there anything lacking in Abbu's house that I'm forced to work? The question is not of need, but of my desires. I have my own identity, my own individuality with which I want to live.'

'Does that mean that my wishes do not hold much value in your eyes?' Zeeshan's tone was somewhat acerbic.

'Of course, they do, and I want your support to realize my dreams.'

When he saw that she was adamant on her decision, he did not say anything further and left from there leaving behind him many things unspoken. He did not come to meet her for several days. Taha felt hurt but did not humor him. Instead, she immersed herself in her studies.

That was her inherent nature. She wouldn't budge easily if she felt convinced about something. She understood that trying to win him over would only mean giving up her studies and her job altogether. She didn't want to be caught in that impasse.

She thought he'll sulk for a few days and then come around himself. But days turned into months and Zeeshan did not relent.

When Taha called up her friend, Shahna to enquire about him. She told her that he missed her, but was too stubborn to admit it and call her himself.

Taha also shared her dilemma with her. She told her in no unclear terms that she does not want to part ways with Zeeshan, but won't be able to sacrifice her and Abbu's dreams also.

'Tell Zeeshan that I love him as much as I love my dreams,' saying this she put the receiver down.

That's how it all ended. There was no further communication of any kind from either side. Whenever either of them met Shahna, they'd wait for some signal, some message from the other. Meanwhile Taha finished writing the M.A. previous year examinations also.

One fine day, she came to know that Shahna's marriage had been fixed up. The news thrilled her for she knew that it would give her an opportunity to meet Zeeshan there as well. She'd cajole him out of his grouse and put an end to their tiff which had unnecessarily stretched so long.

On the day of Shahna's henna ceremony, Taha reached her house a little early. She knew that Zeeshan would be waiting for her. And he was. She met him in the lane outside the house and couldn't take her eyes off him. It had been ages since they parted ways. Her eyes seemed to ask him, 'Didn't you miss me even once in all these months?'

Though Zeeshan was still upset with her, he also did not turn his face away. He kept gazing into her eyes as if wanting to say, 'You wouldn't know how difficult it was for me to live each moment without you.'

Taha had complete faith in their relationship. She knew that she'd be able to appease his anger. She waited the entire day for Zeeshan to devise a way to talk to her, but it did not happen.

It was getting dark. The women had begun to sing mehndi songs, but Taha's mind was elsewhere. She became restless waiting for Zeeshan to make the first move, but all in vain. She had to sort out things within the next couple of hours for she knew she won't get another opportunity. Whispering something in Shahna's ears, she sneaked to the terrace, leaving all the wedding festivities behind.

Shahna too was very upset with the ongoing tussle between her brother and her friend and she wanted them to resolve their differences as early as possible. So, she sent her brother to the terrace under some pretext.

Zeeshan understood the reason behind it and wasn't surprised to find Taha there. He did not show his displeasure by leaving the place. Instead, moving closer, he looked into her eyes deeply and asked her, 'Your ego is bigger than my love for you, isn't it?'

'No Zeeshan, that is not true. You are very dear to me, your worth is above every dream, above everything in life. But by pitting your own self against these things, you are reducing your own status.'

Taha continued, 'It's only when we live together and live each other's dreams together, that there'd be love left in our lives, isn't it?

Without my dreams, I won't be able to move ahead in life, and without you, life won't be worth living. What should I do now? Why do you want to push me in a situation where I have to choose one over the other?' Saying this Taha rested her head against his shoulders.

Without uttering a word, Zeeshan wrapped his arms around her and hugged her tightly. There was no place left between them for any further grouse. Zeeshan understood that it would be impossible to keep Taha in his life minus her dreams and Taha also understood that without Zeeshan's love, her life would not be worth living.

All the misgivings between them vanished into thin air and their new-found love emerged even stronger than before.

As goes the popular saying, "distance makes the hearts grow even fonder." The separation of more than twelve months had rekindled their passion to a much greater intensity. They inched closer to each other. Their intimacy made them both breathless with excitement when all of a sudden Taha pulled herself away and ran towards the stair-case, leaving behind a lingering fragrance of her breath on Zeeshan's lips.

It was the evening of mehndi festivities for Shahna, but its real color was visible elsewhere. Zeeshan's eyes followed Taha everywhere, even on the dance floor. And Taha found herself blushing profusely under his ardent gaze. Their new found togetherness gave her a fresh lease of life.

On the day of the wedding, Zeeshan seized the opportunity and introduced Taha to his elder sister. He then waited expectantly for her to talk to their parents about his marriage alliance.

Yet another year slipped by, as they waited for the right opportunity to come their way. Meanwhile, Taha got a job of a regional reporter in a national T.V. channel, where she worked in the Urdu edition division and was required to cover the local news for them. Zeeshan was quite distraught with her resolve to take up the job but since he was so much in love with her, he had to concede defeat.

They often used to meet at Café Coffee Day after the office hours and then go on long drives. Sipping his coffee, Zeeshan said one day, 'Papa doesn't want a working woman for his son. He prefers someone who would stay at home and look after the family.'

Taha lost her temper when she heard that and countered, 'What kind of mindset is that? Do working women not contribute to the household chores? And, how would my doing a job belittle his reputation?'

'Taha, please try to understand his point of view also. The times are still the same. They haven't changed much. Today also everyone prefers a homely girl for a daughter in-law.'

'Does it mean that you won't marry me?'

'No, I'm not saying that. I'm just trying to tell you to leave your job for a few months. Once we are married, look for the right opportunity and start with it again.'

'No, I'll not do any such thing. You will have to accept me as I am. I don't understand why your father is so against working women? How does my being in job makes me less eligible to become his daughter in-law?'

'Now you see, you have this habit of arguing about everything. If you are a journalist, it doesn't mean that you throw your weight around all the time!'

'Zeeshan, why do you always mock my profession? If you don't want to marry me, then don't,' saying this Taha got up and left.

Next day, Zeeshan tried calling her on her mobile phone a number of times, but she refused to answer. He was well aware of her stubborn nature, so without much ado he landed up at her office.

Seeing him at the reception, Taha smirked and asked him dryly, 'Why have you come here?'

'To meet you.'

'Why? When you don't like me and my profession, why did you take the trouble of coming all the way?'

'Oh my God! What a temper! You know, it is this temper of yours that had stumped me in the very first place.'

Taha burst out laughing and all her resentment vanished into thin air.

'Come, I'll treat you to a lavish dinner at some happening restaurant.'

By the time Taha reached home, it was half past nine.

Her Ammi said, 'Try to come home a little early. By this time the roads also get lonely. We get worried about you.'

'Yes Ammi, I try, but there is so much work at office that it goes on and on. Today the interview with the Minister was scheduled at seven. And it was already half past eight by the time we could wind it up. It was quite annoying, but none of us could do anything about it. And you know, the day's work needs to be completed before we can leave.'

Abbu patted her head affectionately in his usual manner and said, 'It's alright. Don't worry. Just be careful and don't drive your scooty too fast. I want you home safe and sound, dear. It's better late than never.'

'Abbu, our journalist ma'am has become very influential these days,' Rehan said. 'Day before yesterday, my brother in-law's Scorpio got intercepted by the traffic police at the Jagatpura crossing for over-speeding. One phone call from our madam and they apologized and let him go.'

'Yes, my daughter has her own clout, her own identity, her own goodwill. That had always been my dream for you all. It's truly a matter of great honor for a father to be known by the good deeds of his children.' Abbu said with pride.

After everyone retired for the day, Abbu and Ammi continued to remain seated at the dining table. Taha also was about to go to her room when Abbu held her back and asked affectionately, 'We are getting plenty of matches for your marriage. Tell us about your preferences and accordingly we'll get back to these people.'

'Abbu, I also wanted to talk to you about it but somehow I couldn't.'

'Eh, that's good. Sit with Ammi and share what's in your heart with her. I've also short-listed a few profiles of prospective matches, have a look at them too. Decide amongst yourselves and let me know.'

Taha felt elated. She confided about Zeeshan and also showed his photograph. She also told Ammi that his family would soon come over to their house to ask for her hand in marriage.

Finally, the day came when Zeeshan's parents paid them a visit. It was quite evident that they didn't want a working daughter in-law but were helpless before their own son's persistence.

Taha and Zeeshan were ecstatic. Soon their dreams would turn into reality. That night and many subsequent nights afterwards, they could not sleep. They'd lie awake for hours dreaming about each other. Sleep seemed to elude their eyes.

Taha applied for a month's leave from her office but that was from the day of her *Mayun ceremony*. Before that she was doubling up between the market and her office. Despite her Ammi's repeated insistence to take things easy, she did not. Instead, she said, 'I don't want to waste my holidays right now. I'd much rather spend them with Zeeshan after marriage. I'd need them for our honeymoon. And moreover, I'd also require some to appease my in-laws too. Their impression about working women is not very encouraging.'

Ammi kissed her forehead and blessed her whole-heartedly, 'And that is not a big deal for my sensible and understanding daughter, isn't it? Just wait and watch, they'd soon be eating out of your palms.'

Hashim Miya watched the wedding festivities from his balcony. His wife too was with him. She rested her head on his shoulders.

'We are so fortunate that our children are able to live their dreams. Everything is so serene and beautiful.'

'Yes, all of them have chosen their own paths as per their own likings. We have simply stood with them through thick and thin and have given them their freedom, rest everything got taken care of automatically.'

'No, it did not happen on its own. It was you who made it happen. You are the one who has carved out their destinies. They are what they are because of you. You are our *Rehnuma.* Children and I are under your patronage.'

'No, Shahida, no. I'm not a *Rehnuma*. Don't make me one. I'm not the architect of all your destinies.

Hashim Miya got reminded of the last few days before his Abba had passed away. His mother had addressed him as '*rehnuma*'. A *rehnuma* who holds the power within his palms to make or mar fortunes and destinies. He looked towards his palms and muttered, 'I have never held anyone's fate in my hands.' And he heaved a long sigh of relief.

Taha came to her new house as a bride. With her head bowed under the veil, she expressed her gratitude to Allah for bestowing his graces on her at every step and fulfilling all her dreams. She also sought his benediction for making her forthcoming marital life happier and wholesome.

The house was still full of relatives on the second day also and

Taha had to sit with her head bowed and veil covering her face. There were women all around who were looking intently at the jewelry that was given by her parents.

One of her aunt's in-law said, 'Oh, what is this! Is it customary in your house to give merely four pieces of jewelry? And just imagine, nothing at all for your own mother in-law?'

Taha replied, 'Who is interested in wearing jewelry these days? I don't like wearing it at all.'

'What a motormouth of a girl you are! Can't you keep your mouth shut, even today?' Her mother in-law's voice was full of sarcasm as she glared at her sharply.

The piercing tone in her voice forced Taha to lower her head once again when she heard another barbed remark from behind,

'Oh, how does it matter? They have given you a working daughter in-law who'd get enough and more jewelry made from her salary not only for herself but also for her mother in-law.'

The sarcasm in that voice made her mother in-law lose her temper and she exploded, 'You think we have brought her into this house to eat out of her earnings? We had clarified in the initial stage itself that we don't want our daughter in-law to be doing a job, but no one listened, neither these people nor Zeeshan.'

'Yes, Zeeshan is totally smitten by her. Why would he give in to our wishes!' Her *Jethani* also muttered under her breath.

The second day also passed amidst scorn and derision from all sides. And by the time it was night, Taha was close to tears. When Zeeshan asked her why she was looking dejected, she changed the topic citing tiredness.

Zeeshan's happiness, on the other hand, knew no bounds. He was extremely happy that his family had given in to his demands and made Taha his bride.

A couple of more days passed thus, but still there was no mention of their going anywhere. So Taha probed him one evening, 'Where are we going for our honeymoon?'

'Eh, is our Jaipur city any less of a honeymoon destination, that we think of going out?'

'No, my dear, don't humor me with your smooth-talks. Tell me please, where are we going?' Taha again asked him expectantly.

'Not now love, Ammi's is not keeping well. It won't look good if we go on our honeymoon right now. And moreover, they agreed to our marriage much against their wishes, I feel that's more than enough as of now.'

'Alright, but you'll take me for an outing within the city? Maybe we can see a film together?' resting her head on his shoulder Taha asked.

'Yes, of course.'

The next day, Taha had to go into the kitchen for the first time after her marriage and was expected to cook some sweet-dish. She was asked to make mava gulatti, which she had never made in her life. She thought she'd take the help of her elder sister in-law.

'*Bhabhi*, how much sugar and how much mava should I take?'

Bhabhi looked at her sharply and said dryly, 'It's only a question of correct proportion. That is what would decide whether you only know how to make news, or you also know how to cook food. It would've been much better if we had got someone who knew how to cook good food instead of someone who only knows how to cook good news.'

With that snide remark she left the kitchen and went away. Taha wasn't the one to accept defeat easily. She immediately called up her Ammi, asked her the recipe and prepared the sweet dish.

In the evening when everyone sat down for their meals, she kept her fingers crossed, praying that they all like it, otherwise her mother in-law would get even more annoyed with her.

After finishing the meal, they all got up. There wasn't a single word of appreciation for the dessert that she had prepared with so much efforts.

'Ammi, you liked it, isn't it?'

'Hardly. What was it that you made? It was completely bland and tasteless, more like pulao rather than gulatti.' She replied dryly.

Zeeshan also didn't mince any words as he came into the room, 'You could have at least learnt how to cook properly. They are already upset with you and on top of it, this sort of behavior would hardly endear you to them. Don't come crying to me afterwards and say I didn't warn you.'

'Does that mean that it is my cooking expertise that would decide whether I'm a good daughter in-law or not?'

'First of all, don't argue about everything. The only thing I ask of you is to learn how to cook properly, that's all.'

Taha's holidays were coming to an end, but she still wasn't able to enter into the good books of her family. When she tried to talk to Zeeshan about it, he simply said, 'Everything would fall into place if you give up your job.'

'I won't be able to do that.'

'Then stop worrying about it. If you don't want to address the reason behind their grievance, you also shouldn't take any undue stress on yourself. And you should also stop deluding yourself that they'd accept you with open arms.'

Taha resumed her office once again. She used to leave at ten in the morning and would come back by seven in the evening. She had got permission to leave early from office.

On reaching home, she had to hear the constant grumbling of her *jethani* 'You are doing a job doesn't mean that I have to slave it out at home from morning to evening. How can I be expected to do the entire work? You should at least take the responsibility of preparing the evening dinner for everybody.'

So Taha started getting up at six o'clock in the morning so that her *jethani* doesn't complain of shouldering additional responsibilities. She began to work doubly hard.

Next day, she cleaned and mopped the entire house and then prepared breakfast for everyone by half past seven. After that she cooked chapattis for the afternoon meal for everyone.

And before leaving for her office, she said cheerfully, '*Bhabhi*, you just have to cook the salan now.'

'So, is it any small work? Do you know how much preparation goes into it before it is made? Obviously how would you know, you leave for your office?'

After having slogged herself for the house, Taha did not expect this kind of a retort. She was quite upset when she reached her office. The office work itself was no less taxing. She had to sit before her computer the entire day, doing one task after another and many a times, she also had to undertake some field work. After completing her office work when she finally managed to reach home, she was exhausted and simply wanted to crash out on her bed and sleep.

But as soon as she reached back, her mother in-law called out to her *jethani* and said, 'Badi *Dulhan*, you also take some rest. Now that Taha has come home, she'd cook the chapattis. You also are human; the entire day you take care of us all. Let her also start shouldering some responsibilities.'

Taha understood what was required of her. Without saying a word, she went to her room to keep her bag and immediately came into the kitchen to make chapattis.

It was eleven o'clock by the time she finally wrapped up all the work and came into her room.

As soon as she stepped in, Zeeshan came towards her wanting to make love to her, but Taha resisted his advances and said, 'Please Zeeshan, I'm dog-tired, let me sleep.'

'Eh Taha, this won't do. Every time I come close to you; you make excuses. Nothing doing, I'm not going to listen to you tonight.'

Her days and nights had slipped into this pattern. She continued to yearn for brief moments of respite from her hectic schedule. And one day it reached the tipping point. She couldn't take it any longer and erupted angrily, 'That's enough. I can't handle this anymore. I have to work in the house also and in the office also.'

'Who is forcing you to tire yourself in this manner? Leave your job and stay at home comfortably,' Zeeshan said matter-of-factly.

Taha couldn't believe her ears that he could be so apathetic.

Gradually, his love for her began to get overshadowed by the expectations that his family had from her. He probably understood that siding up with his wife would further aggravate their displeasure.

And it was Taha who ended up bearing the brunt of the situation. She turned into an automaton, mechanically doing one task after another both at home and in office without any complaints. Zeeshan's uncaring attitude dampened her spirit. The chasm between them gradually widened and Taha slowly began to detest his advances too. Zeeshan conveniently shifted the entire blame on her and on her insistence of continuing with the job.

Taha shared her plight with her friend with whom she shared a close bond. Barkha also worked in the same office. She suggested that they should seriously consider moving out if it is getting difficult to stay together. That might provide some much-needed respite and save their relationship.

But Taha did not want to take that recourse and alienate Zeeshan from his family. She wanted an amicable solution to all their problems wherein they all could live together happily.

'Look Taha, it's not possible to keep everyone happy all the time. You can't have your pie and eat it too. If his family members are unhappy, you'd have to look for another alternative, isn't it? Either give up your job, or else move out of that house. These are the only two options which I can think of. And moreover, there aren't too many options left for women who dare to step out of the comfort of their homes in pursuit of their dreams.'

'You are right, Barkha, but I won't be able to choose either. You know, how passionate I am about journalism. I don't want to give up my job nor can think of abandoning Zeeshan's family.'

'In that case, do what you think is best,' Barkha warned her. 'But be careful, by silently enduring their mal-treatment, you are only adding fuel to the fire. On one hand, we work for the social upliftment of the down-trodden, and on the other, we ourselves give in to the ills of the society. Do you think that's the right?'

That led Taha to think.

'Taha, take leave from your office, Ammi is not feeling well,' Zeeshan said to Taha one day.

'No Zeeshan, I won't be able to take an off today. There's a lot of year-end backlog that needs to be completed. And besides that, I have already taken many leaves this month, earlier when *Bhabhi* was unwell and then when Papa was taken sick. They aren't kids that I need to sit with them all day.'

That led Zeeshan to lose his temper and he shouted, 'So what? You would have to take leave a thousand times and more if required and not just once. It's your responsibility also to look after every member of the family. The onus does not rest on *Bhabhi* alone.'

'I leave very little work behind for *Bhabhi*. She only has to cook salan in the afternoon and finish one more work in the evening, that is all. Everything else I finish before leaving for office.'

'Oh! So now you'd make us count the number of works that you do. You aren't obliging us by doing that, alright?' Zeeshan bellowed her down and left the room.

They had been barely six months into their marriage when one fine day, her mother in-law passed a snide remark, 'Is it so that you only want to do your job and not raise children?'

'No Ammi, it's not that. We just want to settle down properly first and then later…'Taha replied.

'Don't preach me about all those things. I'm merely trying to caution you. People have started talking that there's something wrong with my daughter in-law that is why she hasn't been able to conceive yet.'

Taha was furious but she controlled herself and left for work.

She was deeply engrossed in her office work when she heard the phone ring. It was Zeeshan on the other side.

'Where are you?'

'Still in office only.'

'Alright, how much money do you have in your account?'

'Hmm, it would be approximately forty - fifty thousand.'

'Okay, I'm coming to your office, I require your ATM card.'

'Why?'

'We ran short of thirty thousand for the shop rental. I told Papa that I would give it,' saying this he disconnected the phone.

Within half an hour, Zeeshan was in her office.

She had to hand over her card to him, much against her wishes.

'You also have money in your own account, why don't you use that? How come you needed my money?' She asked him.

'Oh! So now your money and my money are separate? It is this talk of yours which infuriates me. I have full right over your money, and I'll use it as and when I need it, understand.'

And he stormed out of her office.

The next day was Taha's weekly off. Even on her off days she wasn't able to relax. She had to finish off her morning chores and then wash the clothes. The onus of washing the entire household's clothes was on her shoulders. She found it quite exhausting too as she was in her seventh month of pregnancy.

She had pleaded with her mother to take her home after her *godh-bharai* ceremony. But her mother in-law refused point-blank saying, 'She should learn to get used to staying in this house also. It's been a full year since she got married, but we only get to see her in the mornings and evenings. Now that she's be on leave from office, let her stay here.'

Ammi couldn't do anything except comfort her by saying that she'd take her home after the delivery.

Taha had started panting a lot and found it difficult to work but wasn't allowed much rest because her mother in-law believed that if she continued to work, she'd have an easy delivery.

But she forgot all her sufferings and grievances when the nurse placed baby Umar in her lap. She felt herself to be the most fortunate woman in the whole world. Zeeshan too danced with joy on becoming a father of a young boy. He took him in his arms and repeatedly kissed his forehead.

After getting discharged from the hospital, she went directly to her parents' house in Pratap Nagar.

Hashim Miya was very excited to welcome his first grandchild home. It was for the first time after Taha's marriage that they were all together. As soon as he used to come back from office, he would head straight to Taha's room and play with the little one. He'd be on cloud nine when young Umar would try to reach him out with his tiny fingers.

Barely twenty days later, Zeeshan called her up and said, 'Come back home if you are feeling fine. Papa and Mummy are also missing their grandson.'

She replied, 'I don't think so, Zeeshan. I'd like to stay here for probably a month or two months.'

That annoyed Zeeshan. Since he had become rather unpredictable of late, Taha also stopped bothering about his mood swings. She could never really understand when and what would upset him.

Soon, her four-month maternity leave period got over and it was once again time for Taha to re-join office. She was in a dilemma as to how to manage with her infant son. She knew fully well that her in-laws wouldn't like her leave the child at home.

When she discussed it with Zeeshan, he stated in no uncertain terms,

'This won't do. Why should they shoulder all the responsibility while you have a good time in your office?'

Taha found herself drifting away from him more and more with each passing day. He was no longer the same person he used to be. Now he never seemed to have any solutions. In fact, he was more prone to complicating things. Taha had virtually stopped talking to him. She used to finish off her morning chores without much hullabaloo and leave for her office.

Her mother in-law had started looking after the baby, but the moment she reached back home after office, there'd be a long list of grievances and complaints waiting for her. She would whine and whimper about how much trouble the child subjected her to.

One fine day, when Taha could not take it any longer, she retorted back, 'My Ammi also used to look after him, but never once did she complain. You are unnecessarily trying to show your obligation.'

That infuriated her mother in-law. She told Zeeshan, 'I can't handle your son any more. Leave him at his *Nani's* house from tomorrow.'

Her father in-law also was equally livid with rage. He categorically stated, 'The daughter in-law who does not respect her elders, has no place in my house. You people look for another house for yourselves.'

Zeeshan tried hard to appease his parents but it was all in vain. The situation remained status-co.

Taha herself was no less angry with her in-laws for meting out such treatment to her. Although there were frayed tempers on either side, she found a silver lining hidden behind it. All her problems would get taken care of in one go.

Taha's mother in-law also thought it as an excellent opportunity to liberate herself of all the responsibilities that had fallen on her shoulders and simultaneously express her indignation at the disrespect shown by Taha before her son. Firstly, their presence in this house was becoming problematic and secondly, her elder daughter in-law also was getting more and more irked at having to manage the entire house single-handedly and on top of it, all the extra responsibility of bringing up a small child.

They soon shifted into a rented accommodation near Abbu's house. Initially Zeeshan was a little upset but gradually things smoothened out. Taha also became quite stress-free as all her problems began to disappear one by one. Her parents took over the responsibility of looking after the child leaving her to attend to her office work with a happier frame of mind.

She would keep her house spic and span, buying newer things that would add to its charm and comfort. She saw to it that Zeeshan was happy and contented too. Both of them would often go for a film together. Taha took over the responsibility of managing the entire household expenses from her own salary.

Never in her wildest dreams had she imagined that she was digging her own grave. Little did she know that their present-day happiness would gradually destroy Zeeshan for all times to come and pave way for innumerable future travails.

Taha would buy all the essential provisions on her way back from office so Zeeshan never had to bother about the financials. And since he didn't have to shoulder any responsibilities, he soon became reckless and fancy-free and withdrew himself to lead a life of luxury at home. He gradually stopped contributing towards all household expenses. He also stopped going to his shop, since Taha was there to take care of all their comforts. Initially Taha used to overlook his idle life-style and laughed it away. She would try to coax him out of his habit, but to no avail. He would simply fool around and deftly change the topic.

Seeing the electricity bill on the dining table, Taha asked, 'Oh, who put it there? What would happen if it gets lost?'

'I did. It has to be deposited,' Zeeshan said.

'Alright, then why didn't you do it?' Taha said with irritation.

'I'll do it when you'll give me the money.'

'So, you don't even have enough money to pay the electricity bill?'

'What's there to be so surprised about? If you earn, then why don't you spend?'

'How can you speak like that?'

'Listen, don't lecture me about these things. Give, if you want to, otherwise go and do it yourself.'

Taha did not like Zeeshan's attitude, but she didn't have time to argue with him. So, she kept the money on the table and left for office.

Whenever Taha found some opportune time, she'd try to prevail upon Zeeshan to attend to his shop more regularly and contribute to the household expenses but all in vain. He would give in to her persuasions temporarily and attend work for a couple of days before reverting to his old habits once again.

Taha continued to urge, inspire and humor him. He'd listen to her but act as per his own sweet will which left her immensely frustrated.

Towards the end of her second pregnancy, Taha shifted to her mother's house. Zeeshan would drop in occasionally and have his food there. There were times too when he'd not call her for days together to check her well-being. And when Taha would call him on his mobile phone, he'd tell her dotingly, 'Don't worry about me. You take care of yourself.'

Even after becoming a father of two sons, there wasn't much change that came over him. His habits were still the same. He did not give any importance to the fact that he too should contribute towards the household expenses. The entire onus still rested on Taha's shoulders alone. She was caught between looking after her two sons, Umar and Munaf on one hand and the endless office-work on the other. And to top it all, Zeeshan's recklessness and indifference only aggravated her irritation. This led to frequent fights between the two of them.

Hashim Miya also noticed the growing rift in their relationship, but refrained from pointing it out. He felt if he interfered, things might spiral out of control but at the same time, he was also worried about Taha's growing exasperation. She'd come home tired and take out her frustration on her two children.

Zeeshan derived strange pleasure in pulling her down. One day, sitting at the dining table he made fun of her and said, 'I feel that you are gradually going crazy.'

Taha glared at him angrily and said, 'And who's responsible for it all?'

'It is you, it's your own devious mind that is responsible. If you want, things can really run smoothly. I don't know why, but you get annoyed with me all the time and then kick up storm unnecessarily.'

'You very well know the reason behind it, isn't it? Have you ever tried to understand my feelings?'

'Alright, so tell me, what's wrong in taking life easy? Why do we both need to work? We don't want to become millionaires, do we?'

'Zeeshan, what I don't like is the fact that you are completely dependent on my salary. Why don't you take over the responsibilities of the house?'

'Alright, then you give up your job and look after the house. I'll go out and earn whatever money that I can and whichever way that I want.' He retorted back nonchalantly.

'What's wrong with you Zeeshan? Why can't you be your old self once again? Look at the children, they also are growing older by the day and they also get affected by whatever goes in the house. If they go out and talk about these things, it would be so embarrassing, wouldn't it be?'

'True, so don't nag me all the time. It is these journalism awards that you get every other day, that have gone into your head. You've begun to look down upon me. The day you free yourself of this mindset, our life would come back on track. God forbid, but what would happen if one day you, who enjoy being in the midst of all the news, may end up becoming news yourself?' Zeeshan cocked a snook at her and left.

And that irked her immensely. Its sting was even more agonizing than his actual beatings. Yes, he did sometimes get violent and hit her after some heated arguments, but that did not hurt as much as did the disdain in his voice. It made her mad.

Gradually Taha found it increasingly difficult to keep Zeeshan's various transgressions under wraps.

To the world, they presented an enviable life complete with marital bliss. People knew theirs was a love marriage and that Zeeshan supported his wife in all her endeavors. Taha also very diligently kept the gripes and grievances of her personal life separate from her professional life.

Zeeshan too behaved in an equally suave manner always wearing his winsome smile. Whenever they used to go out, he'd always play a loving and courteous husband, so much so that the onlookers would get completely taken in by his charm. They used to feel envious of their relationship.

Despite all the upheavals in her personal life, Taha managed to purchase the very house where they used to stay on rent. But happiness still eluded her. The brick-and-mortar house appeared more of a prison-house to her since it lacked the warmth of her husband's love.

Taha had earned a name for herself. People had started recognizing her. And that itself became problematic. Her own reputation proved to be a roadblock that prevented her from taking some harsh decisions. Neither could she confide in anyone, for if she did, it would necessarily mean compromising her own status too.

Moreover, she didn't want to become a butt-of-joke before all those relatives who had expressed their reservations at the time of her marriage and were against Abbu for having consented to their alliance. They would get a ready-made opportunity to deride him. She found herself trapped in an unenviable situation where she could neither share her plight with her family nor rid herself of Zeeshan.

The utter helplessness of being forced to endure her husband's eccentricities, despite being financially independent wherein she could bring up her two children all by herself, began to gnaw at her inwardly.

Taha ignored all his follies and continued in full earnestness to persuade him to realize his own responsibilities towards the house and family, but Zeeshan was like a man possessed, he would leave no stone unturned to harass her every time.

'Zeeshan my love, don't you love me anymore?'

'Who said that? I love you as much today as I used to love you earlier.'

'Then what has come over you? Why are you drifting away from me? Why do you enjoy annoying me?'

'I don't do anything of the sort. You know, I always try to find my happiness in your happiness.'

Taha was pleasantly surprised to hear that. She looked into his eyes disbelievingly, only to find that his words and his feelings did not match at all. She said, 'Then why don't you join hands with me for a better and more fulfilling life ahead?'

'First of all, don't try and trap me with your fancy jargon. And secondly, shed off your haughty exterior and you'd notice that I'm with you always and in every situation, come what may.'

'Then why is it not visible to me, Zeeshan?'

'How would I know? Now stop pestering me with your silly talks.'

'Just tell me once, why can't I see your love anymore?' Taha probed again.

'You'll only see it when you free yourself from the fancy luncheons with your men friends in swanky restaurants of the five-star hotels.'

'Zeeshan…' Taha shrieked loudly and clenched her fists. She was livid with rage as she glared at him incredulously.

'Yes, the truth hurts, isn't it? It's tit for tat. How about your own behavior when you try to run me down, day-in and day-out? You always hold the mirror to me, but when I do it, you want to hit me?'

'Zeeshan…you cannot throw such a horrid allegation at me.' Taha's voice was still quivering with rage.

'I am a journalist and all that is part of my job. All events take place in hotels and naturally I have to go there to cover them, isn't it?' controlling her temper, Taha tried to drive some sense into him.

'Yes, I'm a fool. You expect me to keep my mouth shut even after seeing you flirt around with other men!'

'Enough Zeeshan, I won't tolerate this accusation of yours.' Taha raised her finger to warn him. That maddened him excessively. He caught it angrily and twisted it around hard.

'Accusation? Your mobile phone keeps ringing day and night and besides there is no dearth of messages too. You don't allow me to even touch your phone. And if you still want me to keep my mouth shut, then I'll do it, but only on one condition. You also keep your mouth shut. Let me live as I want to live. If you interfere in my life, I won't spare you either.'

Zeeshan's words hit her self-esteem, lacerating her to the very core of her heart. Her face contorted with pain and disgust as she smarted under his violent verbal onslaught.

'Never have I seen a more self-centered and despicable man than you.'

Embittered by her anger Taha retorted sharply when she felt a stinging slap across her cheeks. She burst into tears.

Zeeshan felt placated by her tears and he stormed out of the room with his characteristic sardonic sneer. Crushed and vanquished Taha lay on her bed, lamenting the demise of her love.

Zeeshan had not only broken her heart to pieces but had also ripped apart her pride.

***

The first time I met Taha *Baji* was in Hotel Marriott. It was our P.R. Company that had organized the first food festival when the Hotel was inaugurated.

I was given the responsibility to invite and look after the journalists. At our first meeting itself there had developed a close bond between the two of us. She was so full of life that I couldn't help but be impressed by her effervescence.

The pull of her personality was such that it invariably drew people closer to her. The radiance on her face, her clear full-throttled laughter and her extreme forthrightness gave a touch of uniqueness. The plain silk kurta with a batik-printed dupatta and churidar pajamas added oodles of grace to her personality. Besides, her fair complexion and eloquent kohl-lined eyes exuded warmth and candor. I felt good meeting her.

We began to meet each other quite frequently. Her incredible energy levels and her novel method of understanding things and communicating them across were what drew me to her. She soon became my role model. I used to talk about her to my office colleagues also.

I also came to know that she was no less than a celebrity, always surrounded by young girls who were highly impressed by her life's philosophy and wanted to emulate her and become journalists too. They would follow her everywhere and she also would share with them the intricacies of the life of a working woman with full assertiveness. Her radical ideas inspired the youngsters to such an extent that many had begun contemplating taking up cudgels against their narrow-minded families and live life on their own terms.

Taha *Baji* also worked as a visiting faculty at the University, where she used to take some classes of Journalism course. She had many ardent followers there too. One of them was Sheeba, who used to follow her like a shadow. Against the wishes of her own family, she had enrolled herself as a junior intern with the same channel where Taha *Baji* used to work as a senior editor.

Whenever Taha *Baji* and I met, Sheeba always used to be there with her which gave me the opportunity to know her as well. She was about twenty-two or twenty-three years old. Since she had been a student of Taha, her temperament was likewise quite radical. Whenever there arose any question about women or women's rights, she'd support and defend it with full gusto.

'Eh Sheeba, aren't you ashamed of yourself making a mockery of your father's reputation?' Ammi scoffed at Sheeba as she stood in front of the mirror.

'How come? What reputation of yours is getting tarnished by a mere job of mine?'

'Do you know that our relatives have started telling tales about you? Or don't you? Have you closed your ears; can't you hear anything? You dim-witted girl, did we give you birth so that one day you force this humiliation on us?'

'I am extremely sorry to hear that you are more concerned about what the others have to say rather than about your own daughter's wishes. If their talks could carve out a better future for me, I'd be happy to sit at home.'

'You only know how to answer back. We felt that education would make you more sober and courteous, but we were so mistaken. We never imagined that you'd tarnish our goodwill forever.'

'Ammi, I am setting out to earn a goodwill for myself and not to tarnish your image. And I don't like you stalling my efforts day after day,' saying this she stormed out of the house.

'May that Taha rot in hell! She has led astray my obedient daughter. God alone knows what spell she has cast on her that she follows her blindly. She doesn't listen to anyone any more. They sit with menfolk the entire day. How can they equal men?'

Taha had indeed influenced Sheeba and the likes of her to take up cudgels against their family. She wanted to drag them out of the grim inner recesses of their houses where they had been holed up for generations, especially the girls of her own community. She was well aware of how these multitudes were still living in the dark ages and how petrified they all felt about stepping into the light, often times threatened by their own family members.

Whenever she found time away from her busy office schedule, we would meet and talk at length about current affairs, about life in general and most importantly about the fate of women the world over.

One day, she rang me up and said, 'Anam, come over to EP with Mahira. We'd watch a film together with our children.'

Since it was my off day at work, it didn't pose much of a problem for me to join in.

When we came out after watching the afternoon show, all the three children, Umar, Munaf and Mahira had become good friends. Like their mothers, they too bonded well and chatted happily and unreservedly.

When I asked her why did she not come to watch the film with her husband, she replied rather dryly, 'Isn't it enough that I'm staying with him in the same house...'

Although it seemed like an innocent rejoinder but behind her happy demeanor, I could sense some deep-rooted grief spilling out.

We were just friends, weren't very close till then, still she had confided that much in me. It was probably her first step towards being a close confidant and a good friend. She used to phone me often and call me over to meet her.

'I don't know why, but I see in you a good friend in whom I can confide anything and everything.' She would smile and then herself provide the reason too.

'You are neither related to my family that you would snigger at my helplessness, nor are you from my office where people are envious of my success. You wouldn't carry my tales anywhere, probably that is why I feel safe in sharing my miserable plight with you.'

Her confession did indeed stun me.

She was at the peak of success, yet so lonely. So lonely that she could not call out to anyone at all. She could not lay bare her heart before any of her brothers or sisters or cousins or parents or friends and reveal how knotted it had become. The reddish hue of her blood had increasingly turned murky and with every breath that she took, it had begun to seep inside her system. I was afraid that one day her entire being would get consumed by its murkiness.

It is not easy to breathe in the dark, especially when the life-supporting oxygen is scarce, but she was an extremely spirited woman. She had the tenacity to challenge and raze down all the dark shadows that loomed large in her life. But for how long could she sustain herself against the formidable forces that were bent on destroying her very existence?

It had started taking toll on her health. The tiredness had become quite evident even in her conversations. She seemed quite vulnerable and defenseless now. I knew she could confide in me because as she herself had mentioned earlier that I did not fall in neither of the category of people: people who would either make fun of her or would be jealous of her success.

And it is also true that despite living amidst a plethora of relatives, we can open our hearts more easily to strangers. When we are with our friends and relatives, we find ourselves caught in the image that we have created for ourselves. We are not able to confide in them also because we don't want them to suffer. Same was the case with Taha *Baji* too.

Her parents were happy because she had achieved everything that she had ever wanted to in her life. On the professional front, she had a thriving career wherein she had earned a name for herself. On the personal front, she had married the love of her life and had become mother of two young boys. In other words, she led an ideal life. But it was within the boundaries of this so-called ideal life that Taha found herself trapped. And howsoever badly she wanted to, she couldn't break free of that image.

And how could she have done it? If she did, she'd only end up wounding the hearts that loved her.

Her parent's house was just a block away from hers, but they too did not have the slightest inkling of the angst behind her vivacious laughter. Or probably she herself had concealed her feelings so wonderfully well, that her family remained oblivious to what lay behind that happy façade.

Though she was surrounded by friends and relatives, she was very lonely from within and this loneliness was gradually devouring her.

It was nearly after three months that I met her again at a press-meet of a jewelry show. Both of us had got so engrossed in my own lives that neither of us connected with the other. I was a trifle conscious too of the fact that I should have checked on her well-being.

She looked visibly tired. Her eyes seemed to have sunken and there were dark circles around them too. But she still looked pretty, despite the signs of exhaustion. Her new hair-cut suited her quite well. And in her characteristic round-neck kurta she looked like an accomplished writer.

As soon as the conference was over, we met for lunch and her opening sentence was, 'What a liar you are! You call me "*Baji*", but you didn't even bother to call me once to find out how I was.'

'Why what happened? Is everything alright?'

'Yes, I'm fine now. You know I had brain tumor.' Striking a balance between her feigned anger for not being in touch earlier and her usual characteristic ease, she apprised me of her grave illness as if it was some ordinary flu or congestion that she was referring to.

My eyes widened with fear and I could just utter, 'What?'

She looked at the expressions on my pale face and smiled reassuringly. 'Anam, I'm fine now. Don't worry. I've got it operated and removed.' She said and patted my shoulders.

Oh, no wonder, she was on leave!

'Why didn't you tell me? When did you have the operation?'

'I had gone to Gurgaon, got it done there itself. I joined back office after a couple of months of leave. And it's just been a week since I started with field trips again,' she elaborated.

I wasn't as accomplished a person as Taha *Baji* that I could conceal my anguish behind a façade of cheerfulness. I clasped her hands tightly as tears began to roll down my cheeks.

'Oh, don't cry. I'm still alive and kicking. Look, I'm very much here in front of you.' She gave me a warm hug and began to share her experiences. 'You know, I was absolutely fed-up sitting at home. I've got so used to working that when I had to stay at home, I felt rudderless. I felt myself go adrift. I only found solace in my sons' presence around the house, but once they were off to school, I didn't know how to pass time.'

'Do you know, Anam, when a woman crosses the threshold of her house to work outside, leave aside the relatives, her own home also becomes a stranger? It refuses to make her feel welcome. It fails to provide any succor. It used to be my dream-home once for which I had saved every penny so diligently, today it no longer holds my interest.'

'No *Baji*, don't say that. It's your own house and there is peace and comfort there for you. It's the question of mere perspective. Don't let these setbacks overwhelm you, you'd soon find the same house inviting.'

'Are you trying to placate me?'

I lowered my eyes. Little did I know how to console so perceptive a person like her.

'Anam, how can you say that? How can a house be still inviting if there is no love left there? Anyways, let's leave it at that. I really wanted to have a heart-to-heart chat with you, but somehow couldn't call you...'

She paused for a while, so I asked her, 'You are fine now, isn't it? There is nothing to worry, is there?'

'Yes, everything is fine.' she replied. 'Anam, do you know, even Zeeshan has become more pliant now that he's seen me struggling for life. He took good care of me and also of the kids.'

She continued, 'Maybe he was scared to see me that way. He must have thought what would happen to him and children if I die. He is no longer used to working for a living.' And she guffawed loudly.

I found myself struggling hard to fathom the depth of her pain behind that full-throttled laughter.

'Okay, let's forget about these things. Do you know, next month I'm being given the best journalist award in Delhi?'

I felt extremely happy in her happiness and congratulated her from the core of my heart and also wished for a healthy life ahead for her.

'Alright, I have to go now. I'll see you later. There is so much that I want to share with you.' And she left, leaving behind her a whole lot of unanswered questions for me again.

'Everyone expects love and compassion from their loved ones, God alone knows who would *Baji* expect it from?'

None of her friends and relatives had the slightest clue about her plight. Little did they know that she, who had always insisted on carving a niche for herself in this predominantly men's world, was so deeply scarred herself. The tentacles of patriarchy had entangled her from all sides and she found herself succumbing to it slowly. Although she was not the kind of person who could be cowed down easily, but her own people did not leave any stone unturned to crush her. At every step, they stalled her progress and did not let her triumph.

'People believe that she's leading a happy and successful life. Let that turn into a reality. Please God, I pray to you from the very core of my heart.'

Taha's whole life was a glaring illustration of how men begin to stake their claims at being Godheads, the all-powerful ones, as soon as they become husbands.

Why do these Godheads impose their own terms and conditions on others? Why do they want people to conduct themselves only as per their wishes! Why don't they show some magnanimity and write only good things in their destinies? Why can't they be like fathers, whose soul desire is the ultimate happiness of his children?

These were the questions that had begun to hound me.

I had the good fortune of meeting *Baji* again at another conference. She had confided in me then, 'Anam, I get so furious with him these days, that I feel like murdering him.' And she had clenched her teeth. 'Had I not been bothered Abbu's reputation or about the promise that I had made to myself, I would have divorced him long back.'

She was infuriated with Zeeshan.

'Why, what happened, *Baji*?'

'What happened! He just lazes around the entire day and keeps on irking me endlessly. My health has begun to deteriorate once again.'

'I lose consciousness every now and then, but he doesn't lift a finger to help me, instead keeps on jeering at me. Thankfully, my son is now mature enough to understand the situation and he immediately calls his grandmother who comes and takes care of me.'

'Ammi and Abbu also are under tremendous stress. They say, "Why don't you leave him and come and stay with us. If something untoward happens to you, how are we going to live?"

'Look Anam, it's only your parents who are your true well-wishers. They empathize with you in all situations. The husbands only know how to issue dictums. If for some reason you aren't able to comply with their desires, they'd pounce on you and extract their revenge.'

'The only thing that is holding me back is my father's reputation. I don't want the world to make fun of him, otherwise, I'd teach him a lesson that he won't forget as long as he lived.'

She kept on giving vent to her angst and frustration. Her abhorrence for Zeeshan had increased manifold but she still was unable to forge a separate identity for herself away from him. She was cutting short the years of her own life, but wasn't yet ready to pull down the curtains on her phony happiness and reveal the inner malaise to all and sundry.

Her words kept ringing in my ears- 'I feel like murdering him…', 'I feel like murdering him…' I repeated her words over and over again. I was extremely worried about her. 'She's not well. I hope she doesn't take any wrong step.'

Ash-Hadu AnnaLa Ilaha Illa Allah…' the entire hall reverberated with the *Kalima*.

Taha *Baji's* mortal remains were about to be taken to the burial ground. The wailing of *Baji's* sister and mother grew louder as both her brothers, father and husband stepped forward to give shoulder to her coffin.

The father's shoulders appeared too feeble to carry the last remains of his daughter. There was a deathlike silence on his face. His hands trembled, but how could he abandon his daughter at the time of her final departure? He had to be there to shower his blessings on her and write the last page of her destiny with his own hands, otherwise he wouldn't be able to forgive himself till the doom's day.

The brothers who had been so proud of their sister, looked completely shattered. Zeeshan's head also was bent. Probably after ages he had found time to peep into his own heart-the heart that once used to beat for Taha and Taha alone. The heart that used to be happy in her happiness and had jumped with joy when she had said "Yes", the heart that had stopped beating when she had said "No".

Her death had jolted him into a realization that it was only Taha who was there in his heart. In his arrogance of being a husband he had long strangled the lover within. He had slaughtered his love with his own hands…

It was his own apathy that had made him oblivious of the ever-widening chasm between them. He had allowed himself to drift away from his beloved. Drift far…very far. Taha had tried her utmost to drive sense into him, tried hard to bring him back into their little world of love and happiness, but he was too egoïstic to pay heed to her. And today when he was forced out of his self-imposed torpor, he was devastated.

He felt so completely drained of all energy that he couldn't take a single step forward. The burden of Taha's coffin on his shoulders was harder to endure than life itself and he collapsed on his haunches, totally broken.

Sobbing bitterly, he pleaded with folded hands for his beloved's forgiveness, but today she was beyond listening. She had always been known for her stubbornness. And once she had made her resolve, it was impossible to influence her to do otherwise. And today she had made up her mind that she wouldn't listen to any of Zeeshan's pleas.

Zeeshan recalled how she had threatened him once, saying, 'I'd just leave you and go away one day' and he had laughed so derisively at her that she had burst into tears.

That very laughter of his seemed to boomerang back at him from Taha's motionless body. Her piercing laughter resonated in his ears, ripping his heart out. He covered his ears with his palms. Then removed them again to stand before her with folded hands, begging for her forgiveness, asking her to take pity on his tormented soul, but Taha was beyond listening.

How could she listen? An invisible wall had come in between them. It was Zeeshan himself who had erected it in the very first place. Now he found himself left all alone behind it.

As he became conscious of his surroundings, he saw his two sons standing close to him, consoling him, wiping his tears. He hugged them tightly in his arms.

Crying bitterly Zeeshan held the coffin once again. And they left. The entire hall and the street outside reverberated with the *kalima* of Taha's departure.

One more patronage:

'Hello.'

'Hello Anam, how are you?'

'I'm much better now.'

'So, what have you thought? Have you decided to take back your resignation?'

'I have thought about it. I don't want to do the job anymore.'

'How can you do that? It would only mean that you are afraid to face challenges and have accepted defeat.'

'No Soma, I am tired now and wish to take things easy.'

'And what about your dreams?'

'I can't realize them alone, I want togetherness…not the kind of togetherness that ends in a disaster.'

'You still haven't been able to come out of Taha's grief. Everyone's life is not similar, Anam. You yourself say that Alim is so much better than other husbands. Then, what are you afraid of?'

'I'm scared. What would happen if he also changes? Even if I'm able to realize my dreams, what would I do without my loved ones? Life would be incomplete, isn't it?'

'I don't understand you. But I would insist on one thing, think over it once again. Think about your own life, your own identity. What would be left of you without your job?'

'I'm trying to carve my own identity with Alim's.'

'Anam, wake up. Get ready.'

'Why? Where do we have to go?'

'Your office. To take back your resignation.'

I looked at Alim with astonishment. I hadn't imagined this sort of response from my husband.

'Why are you looking at me like that? Your dreams and my dreams are one only. We would live each of our dreams together. You live your life the way you want to live, free of all encumbrances. I'd take care of all the domestic issues. You just look after yourself.' Alim took her face in his hands and said lovingly.

'No Alim, I don't want to work any longer. I'm scared.'

'I understand Anam, but I'll prove it that everyone is not similar. I cannot see you trapped like this. We would live our lives together and respect each other's dreams. Just wait and watch, ours would be an ideal life for all to see and emulate. Now hurry up and get out of bed. I like you frolicking around the house cheerfully. If you want to fight with me, you can fight, but don't keep quiet. Your silence kills me.'

Alim gave me a warm hug and my eyes filled with tears. And as the tears began to roll down my cheeks, all my grievances got washed away. Alim's embrace spoke of his deep commitment and love and I felt secure with his arms around me.

'Mumma…Mumma…look what I'm going to become,' their attention got diverted towards Mahira as she came running into the room. Wiping the tears off my face, I took her in my lap. She had the newspaper in her hands.

'Mumma, look I'll also bring home a trophy one day.'

On the front page was printed a big photograph of Sania Mirza, the ace tennis player. We both could not help laughing. Alim picked her in his lap and began to shower his love on her. She too hugged us both.

'I am going to make all your dreams come true. We would always be together…always.'

The life ahead:

'So, madam, your maid was able to revolt against her own husband after all, isn't it?' Seema said as she opened her lunchbox on the canteen table.

'Oh yes, long live our revolutionary gang. We make sure that we bring about a positive change around us,' Manjulata added further.

'And what changes have you brought about in your own life, madam?' thumping the canteen table I inquired.

'Oh, plenty of them! These days, I don't cry even if my husband beats me. As a result of which he isn't able to find a release he's looking for. In fact, it frustrates him even more. And I enjoy seeing him all worked up.' She retorted with a characteristic gleam in her eyes.

Everyone felt disheartened with her plight, but they didn't want to offset her ready wit with their sympathetic words.

'Manju, yours is a love marriage, isn't it?' Soma tried to humor her out of her misery.

'Yes, those were the days my friend! Sandeep was so enamored of me that he fought with his whole family to marry me. I tried my best to convince him against it, telling him that if our families don't want us to be together, let's not force them. It was at his firm insistence only that I could gather enough courage to elope from my house. Otherwise, it wouldn't have been possible for a coward like me. He used to love me a lot.' Manjulata heaved a deep sigh.

'I'm sure, he still does.' I spoke.

'Yes, he still loves me very much…when he comes home drunk.'

'Forget about me. Tell us, what did you tell Shyama Didi that made a traditional Indian woman like her leave her *pati-parmeshwar* for good? Manjulata tried to deflect the topic away from herself.

The canteen room resounded with their bubbling laughter once again.

'In this entire confusion, we were the ones who were at the receiving end. She left our work and went away. And now Alim and I have to bear the burden of managing the entire household chores ourselves only. What a great relief it would be to find a new maid!'

'Oh, how lovely! Alim also helps in the household work? Then I would wish that you never find a new maid. May you keep complementing and supporting each other this way.' Everyone raised their hands in prayers.

As they stepped out of the canteen, they saw Nisha coming in.

'Hello Nisha!'

'Hello. How are you all?'

'We are all good.' And they smiled at her.

Manjulata also greeted her warmly. After she left, we were amazed by Manju's attitude and looked at her questioningly .

'Whatever she is doing, she is happy, isn't it? It's her life, let her live as she wants to live. At least, she is not forced to shoulder the baggage of relationships under any social pressure. Like everyone else, she too has an equal right to be happy.'

Manjulata smiled as she moved towards her cabin.

Glossary

Azan: The Islamic call to prayer at prescribed times of the day.

Ash-Hadu AnnaLa Ilaha Illa Allah: I bear witness that no one deserves to be worshipped except Allah and I bear witness that Muhammad is the Messenger of Allah.

Baggi: Carriage drawn by horse/horses.

Burka. It is an enveloping outer garment that is worn by women in some Islamic traditions. It covers the body and the face of the women from public eye.

Durgah: Tomb of a Muslim saint, a Muslim shrine.

Dholak: Drum-like musical instrument.

Eidi: Gifts given to children by elder relatives, family friends as part of *Eid* celebrations.

Eidgaah: Mosque.

Godh Bharai: Baby shower.

Iftar: Iftar is the evening meal for breaking the fast, just as *sehri* is the first meal at dawn.

Kuchcha-pacca: Kuchcha is temporary, made of mud, bamboo, thatch etc. Pucca is made of RCC cement etc.

Kazi Sahib: A priest/ a magistrate of the Sharia court who exercises extra judicial functions, such as marriage, mediation, supervision, auditing of public works.

Kalima: Islamic phrase.

Madarsa: Institution or school for the study of Islamic theology and religion.

Maulana: Muslim scholar revered for his religious learning or piety.

Munh Dikhai: The customary ritual when the groom gifts something precious to his bride on their first night together. Or gifts given by relatives when they see the bride for the first time.

Mayun ceremony: The ritual of applying turmeric and sandalwood paste to the bride so as to prepare her for the nuptials. After the ceremony the bride and the groom cannot meet each other until their wedding day.

Mehndiwali: Person skilled in applying intricate henna designs.

Mehar: Obligation in the form of money or possessions paid by the groom to the bride at the time of Islamic marriage.

Mithi sivainya: Dessert made from sweet vermicelli.

Lehnga: Long skirt.

Nashra: Ceremony to celebrate completion of the Quran by a child.

Naat Khwani: Poetry in praise of Prophet Mohammad.

Paan: Betel leaf.

Parmeshwar: God.

Pati-parmeshwar: Godlike Husband.

Purdah: Religious and social practice of keeping women in seclusion.

Raat Rani: Fragrant flowering bush, also called queen of night.

Rehnuma: A Patriarch who is a Guide, Guardian, Protector, Benefactor, all rolled into one.

Roza: Fasting/abstaining from food, drink, smoking, and sexual activity during the month of Ramadan.

Sasural: In-law's house.

Samdhin: Mother in-law of daughter or son.

Sehri: Pre-dawn meals taken by Muslims before fasting from dawn to sunset during the month of Ramadan.

Shagun: Token cash money given at any auspicious occasion for good luck.

Shagun thal: Gift plates.

Sharia law: Islamic law is a set of religious principles which form part of the Islamic culture.

Surah Al Baqarah: Second longest chapter of the Quran.

Suhagan: Married women.

Thokbazar: Wholesale market.

Tika: A piece of jewelry worn on the forehead.

Ubtan: Sandalwood and turmeric paste that is applied to the bride-to-be.

Urs: Death anniversary of Sufi saint Kwaja Moinuddin Chishti.

Relations:-

Baji: Elder sister.

Dulha: Bridegroom.

Dulhan: Bride. It is also sometimes used to refer to devrani, or younger sister in-law or daughter in-law.

Bhabhi: Brother/ brother in-law's wife.

Chacha: Father's younger brother.

Taya: Father's elder brother.

Tai Ammi: Father's elder brother's wife, here Gudiya's mother in-law.

Jethani: Husband's elder brother's wife.

Khala: Mother's sisters.

Phuphi: Father's sisters.

Nani: Maternal grandmother.

Namaz/Salat/Salaah: Obligatory prayers performed by a practising Muslim five times a day facing the city of Mecca. It is offered early in the morning, afternoon, evening, near sunset and late evening. The timings for the *namaz* are dependent on the movement of the sun.

Fajr namaz: Early morning prayers around 4:22 a.m.

Zuhr (Duhr)namaz: Noon prayers around12:26 p.m.

Asr namaz: Afternoon prayers around 3:47 p.m.

Maghrib namaz: Evening prayers around 7.06 p.m.

Isha namaz: Night prayers around 8:29 p.m.

Taraveeh: Additional ritual prayers at night after the Isha prayer during the month of Ramadan.

❑❑❑

श्रेष्ठ भारतीय साहित्य

भारतीय ज्ञानपीठ